Anthony Gilbert and The Murder Room

>>> This title is part of The Murder Room, our series dedicated to making available out-of-print or hard-to-find titles by classic crime writers.

Crime fiction has always held up a mirror to society. The Victorians were fascinated by sensational murder and the emerging science of detection; now we are obsessed with the forensic detail of violent death. And no other genre has so captivated and enthralled readers.

Vast troves of classic crime writing have for a long time been unavailable to all but the most dedicated frequenters of second-hand bookshops. The advent of digital publishing means that we are now able to bring you the backlists of a huge range of titles by classic and contemporary crime writers, some of which have been out of print for decades.

From the genteel amateur private eyes of the Golden Age and the femmes fatales of pulp fiction, to the morally ambiguous hard-boiled detectives of mid twentieth-century America and their descendants who walk our twenty-first century streets, The Murder Room has it all. **>>>**

The Murder Room
Where Criminal Mind

themurderroom.com

T0352526

Anthony Gilbert (1899–1973)

Anthony Gilbert was the pen name of Lucy Beatrice Malleson. Born in London, she spent all her life there, and her affection for the city is clear from the strong sense of character and place in evidence in her work. She published 69 crime novels, 51 of which featured her best known character, Arthur Crook, a vulgar London lawyer totally (and deliberately) unlike the aristocratic detectives, such as Lord Peter Wimsey, who dominated the mystery field at the time. She also wrote more than 25 radio plays, which were broadcast in Great Britain and overseas. Her thriller *The Woman in Red* (1941) was broadcast in the United States by CBS and made into a film in 1945 under the title *My Name is Julia Ross*. She was an early member of the British Detection Club, which, along with Dorothy L. Sayers, she prevented from disintegrating during World War II. Malleson published her autobiography, *Three-a-Penny*, in 1940, and wrote numerous short stories, which were published in several anthologies and in such periodicals as *Ellery Queen's Mystery Magazine* and *The Saint*. The short story 'You Can't Hang Twice' received a Queens award in 1946. She never married, and evidence of her feminism is elegantly expressed in much of her work.

By Anthony Gilbert

Scott Egerton series

Tragedy at Freyne (1927)

The Murder of Mrs
Davenport (1928)

Death at Four Corners (1929)

The Mystery of the Open
Window (1929)

The Night of the Fog (1930)

The Body on the Beam (1932)

The Long Shadow (1932)

The Musical Comedy
Crime (1933)

An Old Lady Dies (1934)

The Man Who Was Too
Clever (1935)

**Mr Crook Murder
Mystery series**

Murder by Experts (1936)

The Man Who Wasn't
There (1937)

Murder Has No Tongue (1937)

Treason in My Breast (1938)

The Bell of Death (1939)

Dear Dead Woman (1940)
aka *Death Takes a Redhead*

The Vanishing Corpse (1941)
aka *She Vanished in the Dawn*

The Woman in Red (1941)
aka *The Mystery of the
Woman in Red*

Death in the Blackout (1942)
aka *The Case of the Tea-
Cosy's Aunt*

Something Nasty in the
Woodshed (1942)
aka *Mystery in the Woodshed*

The Mouse Who Wouldn't
Play Ball (1943)
aka *30 Days to Live*

He Came by Night (1944)
aka *Death at the Door*

The Scarlet Button (1944)
aka *Murder Is Cheap*

A Spy for Mr Crook (1944)

The Black Stage (1945)
aka *Murder Cheats the Bride*

Don't Open the Door (1945)
aka *Death Lifts the Latch*

Lift Up the Lid (1945)
aka *The Innocent Bottle*

The Spinster's Secret (1946)
aka *By Hook or by Crook*

Death in the Wrong Room
(1947)

Die in the Dark (1947)
aka *The Missing Widow*

Death Knocks Three Times
(1949)

Murder Comes Home (1950)

A Nice Cup of Tea (1950)
aka *The Wrong Body*

Lady-Killer (1951)

Miss Pinnegar Disappears (1952)
aka *A Case for Mr Crook*

Footsteps Behind Me (1953)
aka *Black Death*

Snake in the Grass (1954)
aka *Death Won't Wait*

Is She Dead Too? (1955)
aka *A Question of Murder*

And Death Came Too (1956)

Riddle of a Lady (1956)

Give Death a Name (1957)

Death Against the Clock (1958)

Death Takes a Wife (1959)
aka *Death Casts a Long Shadow*

Third Crime Lucky (1959)
aka *Prelude to Murder*

Out for the Kill (1960)

She Shall Die (1961)
aka *After the Verdict*

Uncertain Death (1961)

No Dust in the Attic (1962)

Ring for a Noose (1963)

The Fingerprint (1964)

The Voice (1964)
aka *Knock, Knock! Who's There?*

Passenger to Nowhere (1965)

The Looking Glass Murder (1966)

The Visitor (1967)

Night Encounter (1968)
aka *Murder Anonymous*

Missing from Her Home (1969)

Death Wears a Mask (1970)
aka *Mr Crook Lifts the Mask*

Murder is a Waiting Game (1972)

Tenant for the Tomb (1971)

A Nice Little Killing (1974)

Standalone Novels

The Case Against Andrew Fane (1931)

Death in Fancy Dress (1933)

The Man in the Button Boots (1934)

Courtier to Death (1936)
aka *The Dover Train Mystery*

The Clock in the Hatbox (1939)

Death Against the Clock

Anthony Gilbert

An Orion book

Copyright © Lucy Beatrice Malleson 1958

The right of Lucy Beatrice Malleson to be identified as the author of this work has
been asserted in accordance with the Copyright, Designs and Patents Act 1988.

This edition published by
The Orion Publishing Group Ltd
Orion House
5 Upper St Martin's Lane
London WC2H 9EA

An Hachette UK company
A CIP catalogue record for this book is available from the British Library

ISBN 978 1 4719 1010 4

All characters and events in this publication are fictitious and any resemblance
to real people, living or dead, is purely coincidental.

No part of this publication may be reproduced, stored in a retrieval system or
transmitted in any form or by any means without the prior permission in writing
of the publisher, nor be otherwise circulated in any form of binding or cover
other than that in which it is published without a similar condition, including this
condition, being imposed on the subsequent purchaser.

www.orionbooks.co.uk

On the day that Emily Foss died a motorcycle, ridden at high speed, came crashing out of a side road to collide with the small country bus running between Finney's Bridge and Elsham. The young man on the motorcycle put on his brakes with a screech that brought people out of their houses a hundred yards away, but it was too late; one window of the bus was smashed, several people screamed, and most of the passengers alighted to stand about and await the arrival of the police. The young man remarked, with the coolness of his kind, "Lucky for me I was wearing a crash helmet," and promptly fainted. A woman who said she was a nurse came hustling forward, and soon after that the police appeared and went into their usual routine. The passengers climbed back into the bus and began animatedly discussing the incident.

"Just shock," said the nurse cheerfully, popping in her head. "No broken bones. They're getting an ambulance."

The occupants of the bus made appropriate comments. The general impression seemed to be that it was quite nice to have a little excitement once in a while, since no one was seriously hurt, of course. One passenger, however, proved an exception, seeming to be in a state of considerable dismay. She was a girl

1

of about twenty, wearing what was virtually the uniform of her age group that year, tight dark-blue jeans, brilliantly colored sweater and a scarf around her pretty throat. Her fair hair was worn rather long and pulled through a ring into a pony tail. Her open sandals displayed vividly painted toenails and she carried a ridiculous little raffia affair shaped like a hamper, to contain her make-up and a very slender purse.

"Are we going to be held up much longer?" she presently inquired of the driver in disturbed tones.

Two stout women close by looked displeased. "Someone's nearly got himself killed," said one severely.

"Won't be the only one if I miss my date," retorted the girl.

"Date? Going to the pictures p'raps?"

"Why not?"

The woman looked shocked. "Fancy thinking about pictures when a young chap's got himself half killed."

"Not his fault he didn't finish the job," came the heartless comment as the girl looked at her wrist watch.

The second stout woman had recourse to sarcasm. "Maybe if you was to telephone the cinema they'd 'old up the picture for you."

"If I don't get there in time," muttered the girl, whose name was Dinah James, "I don't know what I'll do. Life and death it could be."

An elderly man joined in the conversation. "If you miss the picture, my girl," he said, "*I'll* tell you what

2

you can do. Go home and wash that muck off your face. I'd like to see any girl of mine going about dressed like that."

"Not my fault," returned Dinah spiritedly, "if you still live in the Ark down in the country."

The three tossed their noses in the air and sat smirking. A city girl. They'd known it from the start. And all that fuss about a picture—life and death indeed.

They would have been abashed to know that this time the girl was right.

It seemed an eternity before the driver swung himself back into his seat and the conductor tinged the bell. They careered along at a good pace, trying to make up for lost time. Conversation was free and speculative. Only Dinah sat silent. "Len," chanted the wheels as they put on speed, leaving the built-up area, "Len—Len—Len . . ."

The big clock outside the Roxy at Burtonwood stood at five-fifty-five. The big picture started at six. The line that had been assembling from half past five had gone in; stray couples and singles came hurrying up to dive through the swing door, take tickets and vanish into the darkness beyond. Only one young man still hung about outside.

But for the wary look in the eyes, the general air of mistrustfulness that marked the features, it could have been a handsome face; the eyes themselves were well shaped and spaced, the mouth, though large, was finely cut; the dark hair, slicked back in the manner of the day, sprang thick and strong from the skull; but there was no repose there, no ease. The dark eyes moved this way and that, swift as a rat's, always prepared for the unseen foe; the mouth turned down in a disagreeable curve as the young man flung up his arm to consult the handsome heavy watch he wore on his wrist. His clothes had seen better days, but he wore them with an air of defiance, and tried to rectify their shabbiness by a flamboyant, patterned tie.

The doorman came up.

"Big picture just starting," he warned.

The young man turned and gave him a hard look. "So what?"

"Well, this is a Theatre; it wasn't put up for weary Willies to lean against," the man retorted. "And I never heard there was any harm keeping a civil tongue in your head."

He withdrew, outraged.

The young man's face darkened. All the same they were—dames, he meant; kept a fellow waiting till what's o'clock while they fixed their faces or repainted their toenails. Took it for granted the fellows would hang about till it pleased them to turn up. This one was just like the rest. Funny how a fellow kept on being led up the garden path. He'd have sworn she was different. Just another game life played on you, and to hell with the lot of them. He stuck his hands in his pockets and, whistling a rock-an'-roll tune, slouched away.

The girl arrived ten minutes later, running from the bus stop, feeling for her purse. Lennie was gone, of course; she hurried inside in case he was waiting by the box office, but there was only the dapper little doorman teasing the girl at the chocolate counter.

"You've missed the first part," he told her.

"I couldn't help it. There was an accident, the bus was delayed. Did—did anyone leave a message?"

"A message? Here? This isn't the Ritz, you know." Then, seeing the distress in her face, he softened. "Maybe he thought you wasn't coming and went in."

"Oh, I shouldn't think so. Anyway, I'd never find him in the dark." She moved disconsolately away.

"Stood 'er up. I'm not surprised," said the chocolate girl. "Men, they're awful."

"Well, you should know."

The doorman picked up the conversation where it had been interrupted. He had forgotten already about the dark young man with the angry face—though events were going to recall him before time was much older.

That day marked a turning point in life for a number of other people in the neighborhood, besides the motorcyclist and the girl in the blue jeans. Among them, of course, was Emily Foss, who, though she didn't know it, was approaching her last few hours on earth. She didn't look the least like the kind of person to be touched either by romance or tragedy, and certainly the first had never come her way. She was a rather angular spinster of sixty-four, and this was the first time in her life she was ever to attract public attention; and it didn't do her much good because she was beyond appreciating it.

She was one of those women who appear so insignificant it is surprising to find that they throw a shadow just like anyone else. She was neat, reserved, watchful, hard-working and ambitious only in the sense that she wished to make two ends meet and simultaneously preserve her own soul. She had spent all her life in the building on Love Street where her widowed father owned a little haberdashery shop; during the last three years of his life, she had kept house, looked after the business and acted as nurse to a man who became slowly but inexorably more difficult with each week. After he died, she thankfully dismissed the girl who had been making a mess of the accounts for almost a year, and took over affairs herself. She was an indefatigable worker, opening on the stroke of eight-thirty, although in that neighborhood no one would dream of crossing the threshold of a shop before nine o'clock, and not putting up the shutters until six, half an hour later than anyone else in the street. If an interfering authority had not insisted on a compulsory half-day closing she would have remained open six days a week. Sunday was the Lord's Day on which she would not even do accounts or check stock. She never took a holiday, was never ill, never closed even for stock-taking, which she did over a long August week end. Every Friday night she balanced her books and set aside the week's take, except for the small sum required for current expenditure, to bank the next morning. At nine-thirty on Saturday she hung a card in the door, *Back at ten o'clock,* and went to the bank. Everyone knew her, and there was a tacit understanding that she should be allowed to reopen the shop at the stated time.

All her leisure was spent in the service of her church, where she was an elder and secretary of the Rebuilding Committee. Her jollifications were its frequent bazaars, to each of which she contributed a large home-made fruit cake ("Emily must have thought she was designing a tombstone for her worst enemy," one purchaser was known to have reported) and a number of articles from stock, choosing lines that hadn't gone well.

She had a radio and listened to the news, and occasionally to a play, which she almost always found indecent or improbable. She lived alone since her father's death, without even a pet, holding that dogs bring in dirt on their paws, while cats scratch the furniture. As for birds, everyone knows they encourage mice. Her clothes were varying shades of brown, brightened up with a purple scarf; she had never owned a pair of nylon stockings in her life, though she reluctantly stocked them, since even the mothers, who should have known better, asked for them these days. And the greatest concession she ever made to fashion was a dab of powder on her nose; she thought perfume was sinful, and belonged to a society whose motto was Drink is a mocker. When you had said that, you had really said everything about her. Hers was an uncompromising, uncomplicated way of life, simply a matter of doing your duty and paying your bills. Most people, according to Emily, were responsible for their own troubles.

"One of these days," Barney Marks murmured to his wife, "Emily will get herself murdered or something equally drastic, and then she'll realize life isn't as simple as she supposes."

Thus is many a true word spoken in jest.

The event that was to put her in the headlines was nothing more striking than a party given by Barney, the prosperous and good-hearted owner of the grocery shop on the corner of High Street, to celebrate his daughter's twenty-first birthday. In addition to coming of age, Rosie was going to announce her engagement to as sensible and promising a young man as any father could wish. He wasn't in the same line of business, so wouldn't be a competitor or look for favors, financial or otherwise. A handsome, ambitious, confident young fellow, destined to go a long way, prophesied Barney. As for Rosie, she was as pretty as any father could wish a girl to be, and sufficiently in love not to notice if her betrothed had the morals of a gangster and the appearance of a gorilla. But actually he had neither.

When her mother said, "And, of course, we must ask Emily," Rosie exclaimed, "Oh, Mother, no. Not old Emily. She'd put a hoodoo on any party. For one thing she doesn't drink and even if Father does persuade her that champagne isn't the same as wine she'll giggle for the rest of the evening and say it tastes exactly like fizzy lemonade, only it seems to go up your nose."

"So it does to my way of thinking," said Bessie Marks, calmly.

"Remember, my lass, she was very kind to you when you were a youngster," her father reminded her.

Rosie groaned. "Those awful presents! And the sly way she hid them around the room and made me look for them, clapping her hands and crying 'Warmer' or 'Colder.' Mother, this is my party. Why do we have to have her? Ted'll think she's something off the Christmas tree."

"Now listen, my girl," said Bessie, "you're asking a lot of your friends your father and I don't think so much of; Emily Foss belongs to a time when I was no older than you, and I'm not going to hurt her feelings just because you behave like a meanie."

"Have a heart, angel face," Barney put in with feeling.

"Oh, all right," Rosie melted. After all, when you were so lucky in your parents and the most wonderful man in the world wanted to marry you, you could afford to be generous. "Ask Old King Cole and the Queen of the Golliwogs if it suits you. Come to that, I expect Aunt Em would be more at home with them than anyone else who's coming."

"Anyway it's a Friday so I daresay she'll refuse," Bessie put in. But to everyone's surprise Emily wrote a rapturous acceptance.

"One mustn't become a creature of habit," she remarked, "and this is a special occasion."

The truth was she was delighted to receive the invitation; she couldn't stop talking about it and moved in an aura of mystery, dropping hints about the twenty-first birthday present she'd be bringing with her, without giving any indication of what it might be.

"From the airs she's putting on it could be the Kohinoor diamond," remarked Bessie to her husband.

"Much more likely to be something out of stock," said the experienced Rosie. "Probably one of those awful plastic handbags. One thing, you can be sure it'll be something you'll never dare have on show."

"Oh, she may give us all a surprise yet," Bessie offered in placid tones. "I'm glad we asked her, she really gets no end of a kick out of telling everybody she'll be there."

And, indeed, if there was anyone within a mile who didn't know that Emily was attending the party, it wasn't the old girl's fault. She even stopped Rosie in the street to remind her she'd be coming. "And I think you're going to find I shall—let's say—sing for my supper," she promised coyly.

"Oh, drop dead," muttered Rosie, under her breath.

Bessie would have been horrified to hear her. So also would that rogue elephant among lawyers, Mr. Arthur Crook, but he never so much as heard Emily's name until after her demise.

Emily's church associates, who comprised practically her entire acquaintance, were secretly green with jealousy. They twitted her outrageously.

"Remember, when you go bankrupt you'll only have yourself to thank," they warned her. "Neglecting your Friday night accounts just to go to a party."

"With drink flowing like a river most likely," said a second. The church favored nonalcoholic beverages, and all you'd get of those at any party in the Marks' house would be drawn by yourself out of a tap.

Emily rose to the baiting like a trout to a fly.

"I'm not neglecting the accounts," she defended herself. "I shall simply do them when I come back. I don't mean to stay very long. Well, it's a young people's party. But Bessie and Barney made such a point of my going and it'll be a nice change for me."

"Mind you're careful, Emily," said a third. "Don't forget the church Board Meeting tomorrow night."

Emily immediately looked serious. She was an official and it was her boast that she had never missed a meeting. The monthly gatherings were held on a Saturday evening when all the members could be free. "I can't think what Mr. Bastable would do if *you* weren't to turn up." They loved to tease her about her importance; she might look like something blown out of a tree, but when it came to method and management she could startle you.

"Oh yes," agreed Emily, and her face changed color. No one was quite up to making a comment—even among themselves they bridled their tongues—but there was a feeling that Emily had a crush on Mr. Bastable. One or two had even wondered in a roundabout fashion if Emily wasn't perhaps losing her head just a fraction.

"She's so keen on the church and this rebuilding scheme—she makes it an excuse . . . Oh, well, poor old Emily, no one could ever think any harm of her."

An ambiguous kind of compliment, really, but they meant it in the nicest possible way.

"Aren't you afraid you'll be robbed while you're away?" taunted another friend. Because everybody knew old Emily's phobia about burglars.

"I've thought of all that," said Emily brightly. "I've told Barney I shall bring my receipts with me, and he can put them in his safe during the party, so if any of you were thinking of breaking in you can save yourselves the trouble."

That evening she was anxious for once to close on the stroke of six. She had even shaken out the cloths with which she covered the counters before she turned the key in the door, hung out the forbidding little sign CLOSED and drew down the shade.

She made up the fire in the sitting room, carefully covering it with dust, because there was a nip in the air and it was one of those endless drizzling days that marked the whole season during that depressing year. Fog had followed during the afternoon and you could scarcely, as they say, see your hand before your face. Still, she hadn't far to go, and if she took the short cut she would not even have to cross a main road. She looked out of the window and decided not to spoil her festive appearance with a macintosh. It was only five minutes' walk and, of course, she would take an umbrella.

She had put everything in readiness, and she didn't waste a lot of time putting stuff on her face or curling her hair. A stiff brush, a pin or two replaced, her face uncompromisingly washed and a faint dab of mauvish powder, and she was ready. She had a special dress for the occasion, a real knock-out of violet cloth with black stripes, and over it she put a fawn-colored coat with black moire lapels, embellished with round brass buttons like marbles. Over her hair she arranged a chiffon scarf decorated with sequins (from stock), and she was wearing some excellent quality gray silk stockings (from stock) that mysteriously hadn't caught on. Her neat shoes were pointed and had a strap over the instep, old-fashioned shoes that had to be got for her specially by Hardies on High Street. Into her enormous leather bag she put her purse, latchkeys, a handkerchief discreetly dotted with cologne, an immense wallet stuffed with the week's receipts and, finally, the cherished parcel containing Rosie's twenty-first birthday present. This was a diamond brooch shaped like a crescent that had belonged to her mother. Some weeks previously she had taken the brooch to her nephew and sole surviving relative, Sidney Mount, who had a thriving little jeweler's shop at Elsham, about fifteen miles away, asking him to reset the stones in a more modern design and to affix a safety clasp. During the twenty-odd years since Mrs. Foss's death it had never been worn. Emily felt it was too ostentatious to wear to church functions and she never went anywhere else grand enough to justify "real" jewelry.

Secretly she envied the girl her opportunities of flaunting it, though in no circumstances would she have worn it herself because it might have given an impression of better financial circumstances than, in fact, she enjoyed.

On her way to the party she intended to make a telephone call. She had no phone of her own, old James

Foss having set his stubborn face against it. "Be at every Tom, Dick and Harry's beck and call all hours of the day and night," he had declared. "Not likely." After his death Miss Foss had made no change. There was a very convenient telephone booth in Newlands Court at the narrow end of Love Street. The street was like a pair of half-opened scissors, the wide end pointing into High Street and the narrow end enclosing a little paved courtyard where the telephone was situated. Dwellers on Love Street believed it had been put there for their sole convenience. Few casual passers-by troubled to walk down the narrow pavement to this box, preferring to hang about on High Street. At the other end of the court was a narrow lane bounded by a blank wall that was the back of the houses on Barnard Place. And on the corner, beyond the back door, was the handsome, trimly kept mansion, as it seemed to Burtonwood, where Barney Marks lived with his wife and daughter. It was possible, of course, to approach the house from High Street, but on her rare visits Emily always took the short cut.

When she was dressed she pulled old-fashioned galoshes over her shoes, opened her dignified umbrella with its duck's-head handle and stepped out in the street. The rain was very slight now, what she called spitting, but the fog was more opaque. The small houses opposite were mostly shop premises, all closed now for the night. One or two lights gleamed in upper storeys, but for the most part the proprietors didn't live over their shops. There was no one in sight as she carefully closed the gate and turned, walking on delicate catlike feet toward the telephone. As she went toward it she was rehearsing what she intended to say; clenched in a fabric-clad hand were the necessary coppers. Short and clear, she reminded herself. The minister had said only last Sunday, "The commands of God are short and clear; He doesn't argue and He doesn't compromise." Without any blasphemous intent, Emily was resolved on this occasion to follow the divine example. She knew the number and the minute she got her connection she would say . . .

At this juncture she came to an abrupt halt. The thing she hadn't allowed for had occurred. The telephone booth was already occupied.

TWO

The invitation said six-thirty and you could bet Emily would be there on the dot. So Barney was able to assure the police in due course they could count on her having left her house not later than six-twenty-five. The Markses were doing things in a big way, with Barney opening the bottles of champagne so rapidly that some wit remarked it sounded like a battlefield. From six-thirty on the crowds came pouring in and the clock had struck seven before he found time to say to his wife, "By the way, I haven't set eyes on Emily. I suppose she's here somewhere."

Bessie was as startled as he. "I never thought—no, I don't believe she came. Rosie—Rosie, listen a minute. Have you seen Aunt Emily?"

Rosie shook her fair, beautifully waved head. "I expect the rain put her off. Afraid of bronchitis or something. Mother, how soon can we start dancing?"

"Of course it's not the weather," Bessie admitted to her husband. "It 'ud take a flood to put Emily off a do like this. But perhaps she's not feeling well. Poor old Em."

"She'd telephone," said Barney, looking troubled.

"She hasn't a phone."

"There's that booth in Newlands Court. What the

16

Council were thinking of when they put one there I can never imagine. Useful for the kids to cuddle in, I suppose."

Bessie agreed. "So there is. Perhaps her watch stopped. It's all right, Barney, she'll come when she's ready. She's probably changed her mind about bringing the money and has decided to do the accounts first. You know what a creature of habit she is."

But Barney was not put off by any of this; he was a big, prosperous, kindly man and he frankly thought Emily's life too appalling to contemplate.

"I'm going to slip around."

"Barney, you can't. You're the host."

"Let my prospective son-in-law act as my stand-in," said Barney. "There's nothing to this host business but opening the champagne, and I can see a dozen chaps at least who'd volunteer for that."

"It'll look so queer."

"Don't you believe it. No one'll even notice. Nobody ever notices the host at a party, until the drink runs out. Hadn't you realized that? She may have had an accident; it's like glass underfoot. Remember the time she slipped in front of the fishmarket and fell flat on her face? Nearly broke the pavement."

"Poor old Emily. She looked like a kid's map of Europe for a fortnight afterwards, all the colors of the rainbow. Oh, all right, Barney, but don't forget your flashlight, and don't *you* go slipping. You'd go right through the pavement, the weight you are."

Barney knew the old girl would come by the short cut, and he hurried through the court. But he never

17

got as far as the house because, as he drew alongside the telephone booth, he saw her, an old bundle pitched down in the gutter, not moving, not aware of him, so huddled and motionless that he had to stoop to make sure it was really she. Her bizarre finery, splattered with mud and slowly but steadily soaked by the rain, made her seem more fantastic than usual. The rain had made the sequins sticky and the scarf stuck to her pale face. But for all that he could see the great dark bruise disfiguring her narrow old woman's jaw—lying there, he thought, she might be seventy or eighty, any age, and he wondered for a fleeting moment how she had looked when she was young. He did not care for the way she was lying, limp yet twisted, and although he bent close saying her name, trying to rouse a spark of response, he might as well have been talking to a corpse. For a moment he even thought that was what she had become, but presently he found her heart and discerned a sluggish reluctant beat; he was less success-ful with her pulse, but presumably it was there—the problem was how long it would stay there. Blessing the council for once for putting the telephone booth on this absurd site, he shut himself inside and called the police.

"It's a case for an ambulance," he warned them. "She's probably been lying here half an hour, and in weather like this that isn't going to do her any good. I'll stand by till your men come."

While he waited he rang his own house.

"Oh dear," said Bessie when she understood the situ-ation. "Isn't that just what you might expect would

18

happen to Emily? I'm very sorry for her, of course, but I don't want Rosie's evening ruined. You're only twenty-one once."

"Thank goodness for that," said Barney heartily. "No need to say anything to Rosie—if she happens to notice I'm not there, that is," he warned his wife. "Say I was called to the phone or something."

It was very cold; he shoved his hands in his pockets, walking up and down, and gently stamping his feet. Once he knelt beside Emily, and tried to make her more comfortable, till common sense assured him that in her state she would not realize whether she were comfortable or no. The world seemed empty tonight, and the rain began to fall more heavily in vicious lances; it was hard to think that not five minutes away his own house was full of vitality and gaiety and confidence in the future and the world.

He heard the welcome sound of feet at last, and the ambulance men came with a stretcher past the two posts at the High Street end of the lane.

"Don't believe in doing things by halves, does she?" said one of the men, as they expertly shoveled her up and ran her into the ambulance. It occurred to Barney she looked just like someone being skillfully spooned into a shelf in a mausoleum. Nothing was lacking but the coffin. A policeman had accompanied the ambulance. After the men had got Emily up, he stood looking around in a perplexed sort of way and flashing his bull's-eye lantern.

"Dropped something?" asked Barney.

"You didn't touch anything, sir?" said the bobby.

"Not unless you count the old lady. Why? Do you think I might have helped myself to the family jewels?"

"You said she was coming to a party at your house. Well, then, wouldn't she be carrying a handbag, if only for a latchkey—and a handkerchief," he added as an afterthought. "There weren't any pockets in that coat. I noticed particularly."

That was the first intimation that Emily's fall might not be just accident.

They searched around, Barney with his flashlight and the constable with his bull's-eye, but there was no sign of a bag anywhere in the neighborhood. They did, however, find two coppers that had rolled against the wall and that might have fallen from the unconscious woman's hand.

"Two?" wondered Barney, and the policeman pointed to a drain close by.

"Could have had three or four," he suggested, "and the others ran down there. Could she have been calling you up, do you think, to say she couldn't come, after all?"

"You want to get yourself a pair of glasses," said Barney unkindly. "Had it escaped your notice that she's dressed to kill?"

Then he drew a sharp breath. "Dressed to kill! Dressed to *be* killed?" He shivered, and not just because of the rain; he was too warm-blooded a man for that to trouble him.

The policeman was still flashing his lantern, but the only other unusual thing they found was an open umbrella that had been blown a little along the court;

some of the spokes were crushed, and the man remarked, "Wind wouldn't account for that damage. Someone's stepped on it. And, of course, if she had it up and was taken by surprise, she would have precious little chance of defending herself. Umbrella in one hand," he went on, "and I suppose she'd have the bag on a strap over her arm; beats me that women haven't found a better way of carrying their money—fellow would only have to snatch—that 'ud account for the mark on her jaw, too. Must have fought back," he added, reflectively.

"A bag thief?" Barney sounded unconvinced. "Taking a chance, wasn't he, hanging about in the court? On a night like this he could have wasted the whole evening."

"There's the telephone booth," the constable pointed out. "She could have been calling up and then out of the booth she comes and he sees his chance, jumps from behind, she half turns—well, perhaps she'll be able to tell us herself what happened though sometimes in cases of shock they don't remember. You say you know her, sir?"

Barney looked at him sharply. "You're new here?" he suggested. "Otherwise you wouldn't have to ask. She's Miss Foss, keeps the little haberdashery in Love Street. An old family concern, took it over when her father died fifteen years ago. It's her life; come to think of it, it's the only life she can ever have known. Poor Emily! Coming around to a party . . ." he stopped. "That's another thing. She was coming to my daughter's coming-of-age party, and for weeks past she's been dropping hints about the present she was going to bring with her. As my wife said, if it had been the Kohinoor diamond she couldn't have been more mysterious."

"And that would have been in the bag, too?"

"Must have been, if she hadn't any pockets to the coat. Sharp of you to notice that. As a matter of fact, I know she was bringing it because she said to my wife, 'I won't send it, it's—well, let's say it's fragile. But tell Rosie—that's my daughter—I haven't forgotten her.'"

"You don't know what it was, I suppose?"

"Haven't a clue. But . . ." and here his big fresh-colored face seemed to darken. "I've thought of something else. Friday's the night she does the shop accounts, balances up the money, gets everything ready for the bank next day. Well, she said she'd bring the money along with her and would I put it in the safe till the party was over. So she would have had that with her, too."

"Anyone else likely to know?"

Barney shook his head. "Couldn't tell you that. She kept herself to herself as they say, but with friends she didn't mind opening her mouth. She might have dropped a hint or even spoken outright. She had a phobia, don't they call it, about being burgled. Couldn't bear to hear of burglaries. That and dying were the two subjects that were verboten with her. 'Time enough to think about making a will when I'm going to die,' she said to my wife once. She and Mrs. Marks had been friends for years," he added explanatorily. "That's why we made such a point of asking her, and why she broke her rule of years and agreed to come, even though it was a Friday."

"Any idea how much money it might be?" the constable murmured, but Barney shook his head.

"Fifty pounds, sixty pounds, I couldn't say. She was the only haberdasher around, so she got a lot of small trade. Funny thing in a town this size, there's only one other, and that's Bertram's up at the far end, and they're a big place, three floors. Well, it's a shocking business, but I must be getting back now, or my wife 'ill think I've been knocked on the head. If you catch the guy and want me to give evidence—though I don't see how I can help you much—you know where I live."

"Well, sir . . ." the constable sounded deprecatory. Barney was honestly amazed that anyone would not recognize him or know his address, but he disguised this as well as he could, supplied the necessary information and hurried back. On the way he stopped an instant to murmur, "I suppose he didn't think I'd knocked Emily out." He looked down at his raincoat; it had fair-sized pockets but not capacious enough to conceal a handbag, not Emily's size anyway.

As he had anticipated, no one had missed him except Bessie. When she heard the news she said quickly, "Don't tell Rosie, we don't want to spoil her evening. Oh dear, why did it have to happen tonight?"

Barney was a man of fifty and used to the single-mindedness of women, but he experienced a sensation of shock at the words.

"I thought you might go around to the hospital tomorrow and have a word with her," he offered diplomatically. "Keep a bit of the cake. Poor Emily, she'll be as sick as mud to realize her wonderful present's missing." Another thought struck him. "By the way, is Arthur Bastable here? He'll have to be told."

"He came in with Mrs. Earl just after you'd gone," said Bessie. "He's over there. You'd better tell him yourself. It'll be a shock to him all right. Between them those two practically run the church. A stranger might forget a minister was in the picture at all."

Arthur Bastable was a little alert man, sandy-haired, rather sharp-featured, for all the world like a small terrier. He was a lawyer and lived in a square white house near the Green. A widower of many years standing, he had a slightly dashing way with young women.

"Don't you let him trick you," Barney would say jovially. "He's not putting his head in the noose a second time. He knows when he's onto a good thing."

The good thing was, he jocularly implied, freedom and an excellent housekeeper.

When he saw Barney he said, "Well, you are putting on a show for the girl. Almost makes me sorry I haven't got a daughter of my own. But we never had a family, Mrs. B. and I. Too delicate, the doctor said."

He seemed oddly moved. "Bad luck," thought kindhearted Barney, who might complain like mad about Rosie's whims and extravagances but secretly, as Bessie well knew, could have kissed the ground she walked on. Barney remembered vaguely that Mrs. Bastable was said to have been killed during one of the first

London raids. Bastable hadn't come down to Burton-wood till 1944. People wanted lawyers even in wartime.

Barney managed to detach him from the laughing group. Funny thing, he wasn't a handsome man and he was a bit under-sized, but he was always a center of attention. Barney got him into a comparatively quiet corner where he told him the news.

Bastable actually turned pale. "Emily Foss knocked out? Are you sure? Isn't it more likely she slipped? She's been getting slightly wavering lately. I did warn her, as far as anyone could warn such a woman, that she ought to see a doctor, but you know her, as obstinate as Carter's mule, whoever Carter may have been."

"Her bag's missing," said Barney slowly. "The bobby and I searched everywhere. And her open umbrella had blown some yards down Newlands Court, just off Love Street."

"What on earth was she doing there?"

"It's a short cut," Barney explained, and Bastable nodded and said yes, he supposed it would be, but wasn't it a bit tricky for an old woman on a dark night?

"Well, she couldn't imagine anyone would be lurking around," Barney protested. "Any sport 'ud give you a hundred to one against finding anyone there on a foggy night like this."

"Yes, I noticed the fog when I came along. Still, are the police sure? If it's a hundred to one against anyone lurking about as you say, isn't it equal odds that no one carrying a bagful of money would risk bringing it through the lane?"

"The bobby thinks she was going to telephone." He explained about the coppers. "And that's the nearest booth. Besides, you've just remarked, we both know Emily. Even on a night like this there's a certain amount of traffic on High Street, and, whatever she liked to think, Emily's hearing isn't quite as acute as it used to be."

"So you've noticed that? At the Board meeting— good Lord, this is going to be a shock when they hear tomorrow night—several times she's got the minutes, well, let's say inaccurate. I didn't realize at first it was her hearing, and Kate—that's my housekeeper, you know—says she's begun complaining in the shop that people mumble."

"She's due for her pension next year," Barney concluded. "Sixty-five she'll be, when she gets it. She's said that 'ud be a nice little nest egg for when she was past work."

"I can't imagine Emily ever being past work of some kind or other. I used to twit her that she'd never be still even in the grave." He shivered. "What a crack!"

"Oh come," Barney rallied him. "She's not dead. Banged her head on the cobbles as she came down. Not that you're likely to see her at your meeting tomorrow," he added. "But no need to take up a collection for a wreath yet."

"Good grief," exclaimed Bastable. "By the length of your face I thought you meant she'd moved on to that better land she's always singing about. If I know anything of Emily," he added, "she will turn up at tomorrow's meeting if she has to travel by ambulance. She warned me she had a special announcement to make, too secret to be confided in advance, though I've a pretty shrewd notion what it is. Emily Foss, the woman of mystery."

"No sense going to the other extreme," Barney warned him. "Even if the injury only turns out to be superficial—and my first impression was that she was a goner—she's bound to suffer from shock, and when she learns her bag is missing she'll probably pass out again. She had all the week's receipts in that bag, as well as whatever it was she was bringing for our Rosie."

"If they've any wits at all they won't tell her that right away," Bastable consoled him.

"And by the same token, it might be a good idea to keep this to ourselves," Barney continued. "No need to spread alarm and despondency this evening. As Bessie's just remarked, you're only twenty-one once; and even if Emily Foss doesn't mean much to the nation she's been more or less of a landmark in Burtonwood for half a century."

Bastable nodded. "I feel 'proper mazed,' as Kate would say," he murmured. "Poor old Emily! Did she say anything when you found her? Give a hint about her attacker, I mean?"

"Oh, she was completely out. Anyway, I don't suppose she'll be able to help the police much when she does come around. Even if she saw this fellow it's long odds against her recognizing him; it's not likely to be a local man. A whole crowd came down today for tomorrow's races. George Pigott at the Seven Moons was saying he expected to be packed full tonight and tomorrow, and there's usually a bit of trouble at times like these. No, I'd say it was a guy trying to do a smash-and-grab, and Emily put up more opposition than he expected. I'm getting Bessie to go over in the morning," he added. "We'll let you know how she gets on. Poor old Emily," he repeated, moving away, because the young people were clamoring to start dancing and he was, so to speak, master of ceremonies and a pretty good dancer himself in his young days and still able to hoof it quite neatly. "She'll be sick as mud at missing all this."

The wind rose later, trees creaked and groaned; the gate of Emily's house swung idly to and fro, clanging against the post, till someone in the next house exclaimed irritably, "I don't mind Emily Foss having a good time, if that's what she wants, but at least she could latch her gate before she goes.

"Clang! Clang! Like a funeral bell," thought her listener prophetically. She had half a mind to go down and shut it, but it was a horrible night, rain and wind and curling veils of fog, so really it seemed best to turn off the radio and go to bed on the other side of the house where she would no longer hear the exasperating sound.

THREE

The party was like the dormouse's tail, it went on and on, and Bessie, that good housekeeper, insisted on clearing away all the plates and glasses and straightening the room before she went to bed. Saturday was a heavy day for Barney, when all the housewives did their week-end shopping, and he was on his premises before eight-thirty. A lot of his old customers liked to see him around, and he was old-fashioned enough to believe in the personal touch, but while he dressed he reminded Bessie about going to see Emily in the hospital.

"I'll call and find out how she is," Bessie promised, and at that moment the front doorbell rang.

There was no sense hoping Rosie would answer it, Rosie wouldn't be up before twelve after such a night. She didn't work in the shop, not she; she had learned shorthand and typing—her idea and her mother's, not Barney's, who thought it rather a dreary way of earning your living, perpetually taking down someone else's ideas and never having a chance of expressing your own—and she didn't work Saturdays. So Bessie went down and there was a policeman on the doorstep, asking for Barney.

"I'm sorry to disturb you so early, sir," he apologized. "It's about Miss Foss."

"Has the old girl snapped out of it?" asked Barney

cheerfully, hurrying down the stairs. "And how much does she remember?"

"Oh, she didn't come around," said the policeman, a little shocked at this flippancy.

The effect on Barney was like dowsing a light. "You can't mean she's—she's not dead?"

"I'm afraid so, sir. Internal hemorrhage, the doctor says. Came down on the back of her head, and then there was that blow on the jaw, that was enough to put her out itself."

"Blow?" repeated Barney, startled. "Is he perfectly certain about it?"

"No doubt at all. Oh yes, this is murder, whether the fellow who did it intended it or not."

"You'd better come in," offered Barney, dazed.

"We wondered if you'd come along to the station and see the station officer," said the policeman. "There's identification, too. Do you know if she had any relatives?"

"I believe there was a nephew—my wife would know more about it. Here, Bessie."

Bessie was as dumfounded as he. "Emily dead? A blow in the face? But that 'ud be murder. Oh, no, not that."

"Oh yes, madam," said the policeman, with a kind of grim gentleness.

"They're trying to trace relatives," Barney told her. "Here, we'd better all come into the breakfast room. Got such a thing as a cup of tea handy, dear? I bet we could all do with one."

It was another of those dreary mornings for which

that year was famous. The policeman came in, taking off his helmet, and Bessie made the tea. The girl didn't arrive till half-past nine, and Bessie didn't want her any earlier, only got under your feet.

"There's a nephew." She corroborated her husband's statement. "Got a little business somewhere, I'm not sure what, though. Elsham, I believe, about twelve miles away. Mount's the name. Emily didn't see much of him. Didn't get on with the wife. She was a foreigner, he married her before the war when she came over from Germany I think. A Jewess, or something. You'll find the address among her papers, I expect."

"No sign of the bag?" put in Barney.

The officer shook his head. "Not yet. Most likely turn up in an empty house or something, but you can be sure there won't be anything in it worth sixpence. I daresay she wouldn't carry much money in the ordinary way."

"Well," said Bessie, "there was the five pounds, of course."

"Five pounds?"

"That's right," Barney agreed. "Her father told her always to carry a five-pound note about with her for emergencies. Say she was stranded at a station when the last train had gone, though it takes a bit more imagination than I've got to suppose that about Emily— well, she could go to an hotel. Or if she had an accident and wanted a car or a doctor—this was before there was a National Health Service, of course—you didn't find it stitched in her corset, I suppose?"

The police rather frigidly had not.

When they had finished their tea Barney went down to the police station with the sergeant. "You might give Arthur a ring," he said to Bessie before he went. "This'll be a shock to him. Can't think how the church will continue to function without Emily."

Kate Winter, Bastable's housekeeper, answered the telephone. "Good morning, Mrs. Marks. Yes, I'll call him. Is it—is it about Miss Foss?"

"Yes, Kate. If you could prepare him a bit. She—she never came to."

"You can't mean she's dead?" Bessie could hear breath expelled in a low hissing sound. "That'll be a shock all right," she went on in an unbelieving tone. "Just to think we'll never hear her voice again. It doesn't seem possible. Hold on, Mrs. Marks, and I'll get Mr. Bastable."

Bastable came on the line a minute or so later. "What's this Kate tells me? That Emily Foss never recovered consciousness? But only last night Barney was saying . . ."

"This is as much of a shock to Barney as anyone," Bessie interrupted. "He's down at the station now."

"I was just going to see about sending some flowers to the hospital. The committee is going to have a shock when it hears."

"It probably knows already," said Bessie. "You know how this sort of news spreads. Probably half a dozen people are convinced they know who killed her."

"But—I thought she slipped in the dark and struck her head."

"She struck her head, but she didn't slip. At least, the

police think she was attacked. Didn't Barney tell you about her bag being missing?"

"Yes, of course he did. My wits are wandering. Bessie, this is murder. It doesn't seem possible."

"Well, of course it's murder. I've already heard someone say Jack the Ripper's come back from the dead."

"Whoever said anything so inane had better read the case history of Jack the Ripper. This is most likely one of those bag-snatcher plots that went wrong. The fellow hit too hard, quite likely never meant to hit at all. If it had been anyone who knew Emily he'd have realized you'd shift Gibraltar before you'd part her from her possessions." He recovered himself with an effort. "What on earth am I saying? The poor woman's dead. I still can't take it in."

"Nor can we. You know, Arthur, I can't help wondering what it was she was bringing Rosie. Still, I suppose now we'll never know."

"Don't say that, Bessie. The police generally get their man."

"In a fog on the night before the races with the place full of strangers? Arthur, I must go now. Barney hasn't had any breakfast and you know Saturday's always a heavy day for him. He's not like some that have every Saturday off."

"Meant for me," reflected Bastable, hanging up. "That shows how upset Bessie is."

The news went round Burtonwood like wildfire. Emily Foss had been murdered, scalped, found lying in a pool of blood, half-naked, assaulted. There was no limit to the stories. Women met each other in the street and said if that could happen to Emily it meant no one was safe. ("Logical lot, women, ain't they?" Mr. Crook was to remark later.) Single women living alone resolved to put up the chain every night after this, only go out in lighted streets after dark.

Arthur Bastable canceled the meeting that night, but a number of members got together to discuss a floral tribute—nothing so simple as a wreath—and after a good deal of discussion it was decided that this should take the form of The Opening Gates in purple and gold with "Peace" done in white flowers at the bottom. The dead woman's nephew turned out, to most people's surprise, to be a man of about fifty, who had a small jewelry business at Elsham, the market town fifteen miles away. Seeing how close he was you'd have expected him to have seen his aunt at pretty regular intervals, but the fact was that they had been for many years now on the coolest of terms. His mother had been Emily's half sister, the only child of James Foss's first marriage; after her father married again, Ada Foss hadn't been able to settle down. She was sixteen years old, a difficult age for accepting a stepmother only ten years her senior, and she'd married when the baby, Emily, was only two years old.

The Foss tradition didn't run to large families, and Sidney Mount was her only child. He'd married in 1938 a refugee from Hitler's policy of Aryanism. Emily had virtually severed relations with him after that. "Marrying an enemy alien," she said. "Aren't there enough English girls looking for husbands?" And she stuck to it that Else Mount had "caught" Sidney to get a British passport. Sidney had never forgiven her, and as for Else, the last time or two that Emily had visited them she had refused to be officially at home. So that, Sidney explained to the police officer who visited him during the morning, he knew a good deal less about his aunt than most of her local acquaintances.

The authorities had had to break into the little shop on Love Street to discover Sidney's address. Nobody in Burtonwood had been able to help them; vaguely they knew of a nephew's existence, but they were all certain that he had never come to Burtonwood, at least Emily had never mentioned it, and on the rare occasions that she had referred to him it had been in tones of animosity.

"Didn't get on with her niece by marriage," they said in reply to police inquiries. "No, Miss Foss didn't speak of him much." Well, it often was like that, wasn't it? It was a funny thing how people often found it easier to get on with strangers—make friends with them, in short—than their own flesh and blood. So far as the police were concerned they might just as well have held their tongues.

Business was quiet in Sidney's line. With the cost of living perpetually rising and one national crisis succeeding another, people buttoned up their purses pretty tight. Mind you, he had a good name, did repairs reliably, and if anything should go wrong was always ready to have it back and see where the trouble was.

His business was roughly divided into two parts—clocks and watches of the cheaper kind, and second-hand stuff. He was a fair man, everyone acknowledged, gave you as good a price as anyone for your bits of jewelry or the silver nobody wanted, and he was a treasure-trove for people buying wedding or christening presents; but he was like his aunt in one thing, he didn't seem to have many intimates. General opinion blamed his wife, a tall dark woman, with the remains of a haggard beauty, who would never completely recover from her experiences under the Nazis and the horrors and fears of her escape. No relatives so far as anyone knew, in England anyhow, and from something her husband had once let fall, the ones in Germany had been wiped out in one of Hitler's purges. It created an awkward atmosphere with Mrs. M. looking so gaunt and suspicious, though it was generally agreed she was devoted to her son, Paul, a dark, handsome, rather delicate-looking boy of thirteen, gone to a boarding school, if you please, which showed you the airs these foreigners put on once they got away from their own countries.

Sidney was in his shop when the police called, tactfully ringing the house bell—the Mounts lived over the shop—and a minute later a bell rang in the shop itself. Sidney had had it put there for emergencies. Else hated coming into the shop, and if she had to get in touch with her husband during business hours, she summoned him by this bell. It had scarcely rung in a year, and as soon as he heard it Sidney knew something was up. He had a middle-aged woman ("Mrs. M. wouldn't let him employ a girl," said the malicious) to keep the books and act as counter stand-in when he went off selling or was absent for any reason. He had hoped Else could take her place when the boy went to school, but Else refused. She said, not without reason, that it would do the business no good. Although she had been in England for the better part of twenty years she still spoke with a strong accent, still shuddered and became silent when the police were mentioned, secretly refusing to accept her incredible good fortune and not even trusting her British passport to keep her safe. As soon as the bell pealed on that Saturday morning, Sidney said, "Miss Fry, just keep an eye on things, will you? I daresay I shan't be long," and went through the door at the back of the shop that led to his office. There a staircase rose to the next floor.

He found Else looking terror-struck and an embarrassed policeman trying to reassure her.

"What is it?" Sidney demanded. He was a tall thin man, rather the build of his unfortunate aunt, with dark hair beginning to thin, and short, square, very capable hands.

"Mr. Mount?" said the police officer. "I'm afraid I've some bad news for you sir. I understand Miss Emily Foss was your aunt."

Sidney's head jerked up. "Was?"

"Yes, sir. I'm sorry to have to tell you that Miss Foss met with an accident last night and died in St. Martin's Hospital, Burtonwood, early this morning. There wasn't any time to contact you," he went on, quickly, "even if we had known your address. And in any case Miss Foss never recovered consciousness."

Sidney caught hold of a chair and stood leaning on the back. "An accident? What kind of an accident?"

"Well, sir, that'll be for the inquest to say, but it looks as though she was attacked and died as the result of her injuries."

"Attacked?" Sidney repeated the word mechanically. "But who—why . . . ?"

When the policeman had told them the story Else shocked them all by uttering a loud discordant laugh.

"Else! This has been a great shock to my wife," added Sidney, sharply. "Else, my dear, go and lie down. I'm sure the officer doesn't require you here. It's not as if you really knew her."

"So she was killed for her money?" said Else, with the same grimace of amusement on her thin face. "Her precious money that she could never bring herself to part with, not as much as half a crown. You would think," she added fiercely, turning to the police sergeant, "that when a middle-aged woman comes to a house where there's a child and that child her own nephew's son, she'd bring a present, a toy or a book—something. But not Emily Foss. Never even so much as a bag of candy, not even a pair of socks out of stock. Very well, Sidney, I will go. But don't expect me to go into mourning or weep for her. You know very well . . ."

His hand on her hand, holding it harder than (he

hoped) the policeman realized, her husband persuaded her out of the room.

On his return he made no reference at all to his wife's attitude. "This is a shocking thing, Sergeant. Sit down, won't you? Have the police any idea who her assailant could be?"

"If it's a bag thief, sir, it may take a little time. If there'd been a personal motive now . . ."

"Personal?" Sidney looked startled. "Well now, I can hardly imagine anyone deliberately setting out to murder my aunt. I daresay she had her differences of opinion with her neighbors, but that's no motive for murder. Besides, if the bag's missing . . ."

"You'll understand we have to consider everything, sir. I suppose she never happened to pass a remark about—well, being threatened or being on bad terms with anyone?"

"I can't imagine her being threatened, but if she were I doubt if she would have confided in me. As you could see for yourself just now, the relations between her and my wife are—were—considerably strained. Miss Foss made no secret of her dislike; she mistrusted all foreigners. Women who seldom move more than five miles out of their own home town are inclined to be exceedingly narrow. And, of course, her own life was a comparatively sheltered one. Naturally my wife resented her attitude to our son. The last time they met, which must be more than a year ago, she let slip something about—er—divided loyalties—in the event of a war, I mean. Seeing that my wife's family was wiped out by the Nazis it was a most heartless thing to say. Particularly as the child was then barely twelve years old."

"Quite, sir. Was that the last time you saw her?"

"No. She came over on the August Bank Holiday week end this year. I never take the car out that day, too much traffic on the roads. She wanted me to reset a diamond brooch that had belonged to her mother and she brought it in person because she didn't trust the mail. I may say that when my wife knew she was coming she arranged to take the boy to a neighbor and not to return until after Miss Foss had left. It's all been most uncomfortable, but I'm sure you'll agree, officer, that my wife's attitude is perfectly understandable in the circumstances."

"Quite so, sir. About this brooch. Did she give you any reason why she wanted it reset?"

"Oh yes. It was to be a twenty-first birthday present to a Miss Marks. There was to be a party to which she'd been invited. As I say, she brought this brooch, wanted it reset for a young girl and a safety catch added. I quoted her the lowest price I could, without actually being out of pocket, but all the same when I took it over, because she wouldn't have it sent by mail, she grumbled, and there was never a word about paying me the expense of the journey."

"Could you give me a description of it?" suggested the policeman. So he described it as well as he could.

"A valuable piece, sir, would you say?"

"You might get twenty pounds on it if you sold it secondhand, possibly twenty-five. Not more. The diamonds weren't of particularly good quality though they were a fair size. If a customer brought it to me twenty-five is the utmost I'd offer, and with times not too good like they are at the moment I doubt if I'd go beyond twenty. Surely you're not suggesting this brooch played any part in the affair?"

"Oh yes, sir. Last night was the day of the party and she seems to have let it be known pretty widely that she would be carrying this brooch, though she doesn't seem to have told anyone precisely what the parcel would contain, and also the week's receipts of the shop."

"And is it your theory that someone lay in wait for her? It doesn't seem very probable. I know Love Street isn't much frequented after dark—oh yes, I used to visit pretty regularly until the war, but since then there really hasn't been much encouragement. The old man, my grandfather, was virtually senile during his final years, and as Miss Foss herself pointed out, there seemed no sense my making the journey; he didn't seem to know who I was. Besides . . ." he hesitated.

"Well, sir?"

"The fact is," Sidney acknowledged, "Miss Foss had told him about my marriage, and, while he really couldn't assimilate facts, he had got the idea into his head that I had anti-British sympathies. My marriage took place in 1938, when the war scare was at its height. I don't know what stories his daughter fed him up with, but the last time I called she told me he didn't wish to see me. She hinted to me that was why he left the business entirely to her, without so much as men-

41

tioning my name, but I doubt if that was really the case. The fact is she was a single woman and she depended on the shop, and he must have realized when he made the will that eventually it would come to me as the only surviving relative of Miss Foss. There was," he added dryly, "not the remotest contingency of her getting married."

"That's another point," the policeman conceded. "Do you know anything about a will?"

"I doubt if one exists. My aunt had a kind of horror of death; you often find it in very religious people, which seems strange. To hear her talk you'd have supposed she thought she alone was immortal. Of course, there is a sort of superstition—I've come across it elsewhere—that if you make a will (or take out a life insurance policy for that matter) you're drawing the attention of Providence to yourself and—well, inviting disaster. By the way, have you any idea when the funeral will take place? In spite of her attitude toward me I should naturally wish to attend."

"There'll have to be an inquest. Being the week end makes it a bit awkward. The manner of the death, too. It can't be called accident. Most likely the inquest will be deferred after evidence of identification and the medical report, and permission to proceed with the funeral will be given by the coroner."

"As her next of kin it will fall to me to make the arrangements," said Sidney, rather uneasily. "I shall attend the inquest if required and in any case I must get in touch with her lawyer. It's an odd thing, but I don't even know who he is. Still, I daresay there'll be no difficulty discovering that."

"Inquiries are being made at Burtonwood," the sergeant assured him. "Of course, if there should be a will she may have left instructions about burial, etc."

There was a bump on the door and Else came in carrying a tea tray.

"The officer will take some coffee," she said. "I heard what you were saying, Sidney, as I opened the door, about a will. If there is such a thing you may be sure you will not get a single penny—not one penny." She clattered the cups passionately.

"Now, Else, you know nothing of this. Obviously . . ."

"Obviously—obviously . . ." She handed a cup to the sergeant who took it absently. "There is sugar," she pointed out. "I tell you, all her money will go to that precious church of hers. I daresay she was in love with the minister." She passed a second cup to her husband.

"That is quite absurd," declared Sidney, but his hand shook as he put the cup down and some of the coffee slopped into the saucer. "In such circumstances I should naturally contest the will. No one competent to draw one up could leave the money outside the family."

"When did she ever give us anything?" demanded Else. "When we wanted help when Paul was ill, what was her reply? 'There is free hospital treatment in this country; why should I pay?' When you spoke of sending Paul to a boarding school, she said, 'How pleasant to be able to afford it. I am glad your business does so well.' You know she would not part with a penny. 'If he deserves to go to such a school,' she said, 'let him win a scholarship. If he cannot do that, then the State school is good enough for him.' No, no, my dear Sidney if you are counting on getting out of your difficulties by her death you are making a very great mistake. Believe me. She would take all that money and throw it down a drain before she would let us touch so much as a five-pound note."

"There's just one more point, sir," said the policeman, setting down his cup and preparing to leave. "Thank you, ma'am. Very welcome . . . You weren't expecting Miss Foss to telephone you last night? When she was found last night there were some coppers scattered in the lane, as if she'd meant to call someone."

"But—is there any indication that she was thinking of telephoning *me?*"

"Oh no, sir. But seeing she can't tell us anything—you see, there is just the chance that she wasn't attacked by a bag thief, though everything does point that way. She might have wanted to tell you something—some danger she was in—you can't be certain, can you sir?"

"I cannot believe she would telephone to me," said Sidney flatly.

"But you're the next of kin. People have a way of turning to their own relatives when danger hits them."

"Aunt Emily in danger," repeated Sidney. "Is there anything to lend color to such a theory?"

"We're still making inquiries," the officer pointed

out patiently. . . . "Well, if you can't tell us anything . . ."

Sidney shook his head. "Nothing. Nothing," he repeated in a firmer voice. "I should say you were barking up the wrong tree if you thought Miss Foss was asking for help. And—do the coppers have to have been hers? I mean, we know someone else was in the lane—look here, suppose whoever it was asked her if she could change a threepenny bit for threepence, and she held out the coppers, and that was his chance. It's only a suggestion," he added hurriedly.

"Sidney." His wife's voice came urgently from the threshold. "It is not for you to make suggestions. The police do not like it."

"Oh come, my dear, you forget. You're not in Germany now."

The sergeant said later that it made his blood crawl to see the look she gave him.

"No, Sidney," she said. "That I never forget."

She picked up the tray and marched out of the room.

"In any case," Sidney said as the door closed, "if she had tried she wouldn't have got a reply. I was up in London at a sale of antique silver on Friday, and my wife—well, she's nervous alone in the house after dark, and we've no resident servant, so she went over to spend the afternoon and evening with a neighbor. I picked her up there about half past seven, I should think it was. I'd have been earlier but for the bus breakdown. But I still think you're wrong if you imagine she was trying to get in touch with me."

All the same, after the policeman had disappeared, Sidney Mount sat for a long time looking thoughtful, and was only recalled to matters of the moment by his middle-aged assistant knocking nervously on the door to ask if he could come down and see a customer who had a diamond brooch to sell.

She was astounded when he began to laugh, and he shut off abruptly. It was quite a nice little brooch and he made a fair offer for it. And he thought about that other brooch, the one the police wanted and that he'd described for them in such detail. That description would be circulated to all local jewelers, but only a fool would try and raise the wind on it in the circumstances.

"They will never find that brooch," he told himself. "Never, never, never."

FOUR

Detective Inspector Hart, who was in charge of the case, looked up as Sergeant Creagh came into the room.

"No help from the Elsham end," he reported briefly. "Not much love lost there, and no confidences exchanged, so that if she did have an enemy, Sidney Mount knows nothing about him. Did you get anything out of Bastable?"

"He wasn't expecting Miss Foss to call him, though he says he wouldn't have been exactly surprised if she had, but his only call that night came about five-thirty, when we know Miss Foss was still in her shop. It was from a firm of builders giving supplementary estimates, and he made a note of the figures and mailed them on to the minister—that's the Reverend Ladd—on the way to the party. That's O.K., because Mr. Ladd got them next morning. He left the house about seven— well, we know that, too, because this Mrs. Earl saw him and they walked up to the Marks' house together. He suggested—Mr. Bastable, I mean—that she might have meant to phone the minister."

"Any idea why?"

"Well, she seems to have told everyone she had something important to announce at the meeting the next day, and he doesn't know what it was—neither

47

of them knows, for that matter. I suppose she could have meant to take Mr. Ladd into her confidence rather than spring a surprise on him. Mr. Bastable has the idea she was going to offer a special donation to get the rebuilding started, but he admits he hasn't any proof, only he can't think what else it could be. The two of them seem to have run that committee, by all accounts. Miss Foss had the idea that if the Secretary and the Treasurer ganged up before the meeting, everyone else would fall into line, and that's the way it mostly seems to have worked out. It does seem more likely it 'ud be Mr. Ladd than Mr. Bastable, seeing she knew they'd meet at the Marks' house and she could have a word with him then."

"Well, could she?" debated Hart. "I'm not much of a one for these parties myself, but from what I have seen of them they're generally a screaming mob, and you'd have to scream, too, to make yourself heard. Have you seen the minister? Yes, of course, you have. I suppose he couldn't suggest anything helpful?"

"Not much," Creagh agreed. "In any case, he was out that night on a sick visit, but Mrs. Ladd was in, and she says that though there were a number of calls, one from Miss Foss wasn't among them. Of course, she may have tried and got the busy signal and then come out to find X waiting for her."

"We can't go any further with that," Hart agreed. "Not that it's particularly important, I daresay, but one likes to tie up all the ends."

("Chap should have gone into the dry goods business," grumbled Crook when he heard this. "Life ain't all that tidy, and me, I always suspect a situation that ties up neatly all around.")

"Bastable doesn't know anything about a will, I suppose?" Hart added. "After all, he's a lawyer, so she might have consulted him."

"I asked that, but he says she probably hadn't made one. Had a sort of hoodoo about it. Make your will and fall under a bus as you come out of the office. Anyway, she was very cagey about money, and if she did make a will it would be with a stranger, or she'd buy one of those will forms and draw it up herself, with two church pals to act as witnesses."

"Well, that can wait," said Hart. "Once the news gets around we shall hear about a will, if there was one, or else find it hidden somewhere in the house. She seems to have had as many hiding places as a dormouse."

"Nothing in that line from the nephew?" suggested Creagh.

"He seems to have taken for granted that he'd inherit as next of kin. If there should be a wall disinheriting him we can look for trouble from that quarter."

The only other piece of information came from a Miss Tremellen who occupied the house next door to the dead woman's. She said she heard Miss Foss leave at six-fifteen; she placed the time by the radio. On Friday evenings there was a program called "Town and Country" that came on immediately after the news, and to this she always listened. The announcement had just been made, when she heard the next-door gate; it made a good deal of noise as it had to be banged hard to shut.

"Didn't happen to look out and see if the old lady was by her lonesome?" Hart suggested.

"She says she happened to be straightening a curtain, and she saw Miss Foss going toward the Court, quite alone."

"And I suppose it didn't strike her as odd when she didn't hear her come back?"

"As a matter of fact, she thought she had. You know the wind came up about nine last night, and a blessing that was because it blew the fog away, and soon afterwards she heard the next-door gate swinging—very annoying she said. She had half a mind to go down and shut it, but it was cold and she was in a housecoat—that's what they call dressing gowns these days—so she supposed Miss Foss had come back in a bit of a hurry —she didn't say she thought she might have had more than a couple of glasses of the Marks' champagne, but I fancy that's what was in her mind—and hadn't quite shut the gate. Now, of course, she realizes it can't have been properly shut to start with, but you wouldn't notice until the wind got strong. Very shocked she was to hear the news, though I told her there was nothing she could have done in any case. Still, she was in a regular tizz. This is going to get a lot of people upset."

"They'll be all right if they stay indoors after dark," said Hart, unsympathetically. "There's no sign of the bag yet, but that'll turn up all right, like a drowned body, though we may have to wait a few days."

But, in fact, they didn't have to wait so long.

They found it on Sunday, chucked into a piece of waste land behind the church; no particular effort had been made to conceal it, and Hart was right when he said it wouldn't yield much in the way of clues. There was no hope of tracing fingerprints, of course, and all the money had gone, as well as the brooch. They found a little plastic wallet containing a radio license and a receipt for a coat from a firm of dry cleaners, and a half-used book of stamps. The five-pound note had vanished along with the rest; the latchkeys were intact; there was a clean handkerchief and a small comb, and an enormous and very festive twenty-first birthday card, decorated with a gilt key and a black cat and (very daringly) a bottle of champagne. Inside, in Emily's sloping, careful, cramped hand was inscribed an original verse.

> When this you wear
> Shed a fond tear,
> Remembering me,
> Aunt Emily.

"Crazy," thought the policeman who found it. "And where do we go from here?" wondered Inspector Hart. The money would have been in treasury notes of the values of ten shillings and one pound and practically untraceable. No attempt had been made to remove the dead woman's wrist watch or the opal ring she wore on her finger, but then bag-snatchers never did bother about personal jewelry. The place had as many scallywags and hoodlums as most small market towns, it had been swarming with strangers . . .

"It could have been a transient," mused Hart.

"Why should a stranger know there was a booth in the court?" Creagh wondered aloud. "It's really there only for the benefit of the dwellers on Love Street who haven't lines of their own, and people taking a short cut. There aren't likely to have been many of them in last night's fog, or someone would have found Miss Foss before. There's a light in the booth after dark."

"You're so right," agreed the inspector. "Still, it could be that some fellow was calling up his girl or a pal or making a date and he saw the poor, silly old woman open her bag to get money for the call. If he saw the wallet it must have seemed a good chance, what with the rain and all the rest of it. She seems to have made a present to all and sundry of the fact that she was carrying the week's receipts."

"That's a fact," the sergeant agreed. "We've seen some of her neighbors, customers and so forth, and they all seemed to know. One would pass it on to another, I daresay, and that sort of thing gets about like wildfire."

"Mount's been told to keep his mouth shut about the brooch," Hart went on. "We may have to wait till somebody tries to pass it. The old lady may be no more than a bagful of bones before we get our man."

But he didn't really believe it. The police are pretty sharp and in fact Emily had scarcely settled in her grave before they pounced.

The inquest, attended by Sidney Mount among others, was held on Monday and was a very brief affair, the police asking for a deferment as soon as the formalities had been complied with. The church, in the person of Mr. Bastable, approached Sidney and asked if Wednesday would be a convenient day for him to attend the funeral. There was to be no question of cremation, the departed considering this a heathenish practice good enough for those who knew no better perhaps, but she intended to be buried like a Christian. The church had no graveyard—well, land was expensive in Burtonwood—but the local cemetery already sheltered a number of her fellow worshippers and Mr. Lark, the inappropriately named undertaker, could fit her in on Wednesday. Sidney suggested Wednesday afternoon, that being early closing day in Elsham, and Mr. Bastable said he was sure Mr. Lark would oblige. It was early closing day in Burtonwood, too, so Emily could be sure of a handsome attendance. As Sidney turned away, a seedy old man caught his sleeve and asked if he was the next of kin. He said his name was Chuffey, which seemed to suit him very well, and that he had drawn up a will for the deceased. It had been made some months before and bestowed everything of which she should die possessed to the church.

Someone said afterwards it was just as well the old

lady had cashed in or her nephew might have murdered her all over again, if looks were anything to go by. Sidney announced his instant intention of contesting the will on the ground of mental incapacity, to which Mr. Chuffey retorted that in his view the old lady was as sound as a nut upstairs, and there was no law that could compel a single woman to leave her money to her next of kin. The pastor of the church coming forward to offer his sympathy to Miss Foss's only living relative was startled by Sidney's reception of his civilities, and tongues wagged harder than ever.

Sidney got into his car and drove back to Elsham. All the way, while he thought of telling Else the news, the wheels chanted derisively, "I told you so, told you so, told you so," till he thought he'd go mad.

"Gossip," said Inspector Hart placidly, "is the policeman's best friend," and so it proved in this case. On the day following the funeral a certain Mrs. Lily Randall, who kept a respectable lodging house in Tammany Street, received a visit from her sister, Grace Penge. Naturally they talked about the murder.

"You want to be careful, Lil," said Grace. "It isn't just the young and beautiful that get bumped off nowadays. Be sure you put up your chain of a night and don't open the door till you know who's on the other side."

"If it's money he wants he's not likely to come here," said Lily.

"You never can tell. Mean to say the police haven't got a clue?"

"If they have, they aren't telling me. I don't like it, Grace, and that's a fact."

There was so much vehemence in her voice that Grace's suspicions were roused. "What do you mean, Lily? Lil, you don't mean you could help them?"

"No, of course not. I mean, I don't know that he had a thing to do with it, do I? Only it's just like I said, I don't like it."

There was no need for Grace to ask who "he" was. Obviously he'd be one of Lil's lodgers. "Go on," she ordered. "Who is he? What's he done? It's your duty to tell the police if you think you know anything."

Lil seemed perfectly distracted. "Mind you, he seemed right enough when he first came," she said. "As nice a young fellow as I'd had in months; nice-looking, too, if he'd give himself a chance instead of going about scowling fit to put out the sun. Come from London, had a job at the Porchester Hotel. Well, that's respectable enough. The Mayor of Elsham stayed there when he came over to open the new Hall in the spring. I made his room ever so nice—not the Mayor's, of course, this young fellow's—and took him up a cup of tea first thing. You like to have regular lodgers, and a man's less trouble than a woman as a rule. And then I thought, he'll be out all day. . . . Mind you, I did think his hours were a bit funny, but then he explained how in a hotel you're on a shift system, late one day and early the next, and seeing he paid the rent and didn't bring girls home I didn't worry. Then he started making excuses, he'd had to buy a jacket, couldn't get credit not being known, see, and could I wait a week? He paid the next week for the week before, so that still left a week owing. Then it was another week and then it came out he'd left the Porchester, you wouldn't speak to a dog the way they talked to him . . . I had to remind him I had my living to get, too, but he said he had the promise of another job."

"You should have got rid of him right away, dear. That kind's no good. I'm sorry for his wife," she added.

"He hasn't got a wife. Leastways . . ."

"If he hasn't now, he will. Well, he's got to get his rent paid somehow, hasn't he? Why don't you tell him to go?"

"I would, Grace, but there's something about him, and you do read such awful things in the papers. And then—this is what I was coming to—he came marching in that Saturday night, the very day the poor old girl passed on, and said, 'Got change for a five-pound note?' You could have knocked me down with a feather. 'Why, have you found a bank where they grow?' I asked him. He put it on the table, and he asked for a receipt. 'So you've got a job,' I said, and he laughed and said, 'Only fools work themselves to death. Had a good day at the races. Better than being ordered around from morning till night.' And Grace, I saw his wallet and it was stuffed with money. Well, what would you think?"

"I know what I think," said Grace energetically. "You ought to go to the police, Lil. If you don't I wouldn't blame that poor woman if she haunted you for the rest of your life."

"But, Grace, there isn't any proof he had a hand in that."

"Then let him show it. He's only got to tell the police where the money came from . . ."

"He said the races."

"Well, then, someone will have seen him there or he'll have gone with a friend. . . . Where did he get the money to go to the races anyway, if he couldn't pay your rent?"

"I suppose that's where his wages went. You can't teach people these days. Easy money, something for nothing, that's the idea, not work for it the way you and me were brought up. All the same, Grace, the police—I mean people do make money on horses."

"In the pictures," Grace agreed. "Well, please yourself, Lil, but I know I wouldn't sleep easy of a night knowing I might have a murderer under my roof."

As she left the house about an hour later she all but cannoned into a young man who was coming in. She waited for him to give way, but he just stood there, glowering.

"Sorry I'm transparent," he said at last, pushing past her. "Shan't be wanting any tea, Ma," he added to Lil. "Got to meet a friend."

Grace drew a sharp breath; the young fellow was all spruced up—to use her expression—with wide shoulders, narrow waist, gaudy tie, a real flasher. Not the kind you'd expect to find under Lil's roof, and really the girl should have her head examined, keeping him there five minutes after she'd heard he'd lost his job.

"Wouldn't surprise me to know he'd helped himself from the till, and that's why they gave him his walking papers," she reflected.

"Get your hat, Lil," she said in commanding tones, as the young man vanished around the bend of the staircase. "I'll come with you to the police this minute. I wouldn't sleep a wink knowing he was here under your very roof."

Lil protested feebly, but she didn't stand an earthly chance. Twenty minutes later the two sisters swept into the police station.

The officer in charge was coolly kind, but Grace saw indignantly that they didn't think a lot of her story.

"You might be glad of a bit of help seeing you're flummoxed," she observed in sharp tones, having been taught by life that you have to stand up for yourself. "For all you know, my sister's life's in danger . . ."

"Oh, Grace," protested Lil, but she might as well have sat with King Canute and tried to stop the incoming tide.

"I'm concerned for my sister's life if you're not," she told them. "I've seen this young fellow, and if he got that money honestly I'm the Duchess of Windsor. Those clothes," she shuddered. "Brand-new, didn't you say, Lil, since the old lady's gone. Silk shirt and suede shoes, and only a few days earlier he couldn't pay the rent."

It was a trivial detail recalled by Lily Randall that really got the police on their toes.

"And he's gone and bought himself a pencil," she said. "One of the kind that screw up and down. Real silver and his initials on it."

The station officer looked up sharply. "Silver?" he said.

"That's what my sister told you," snapped Grace.

"That's funny," the officer conceded. "With that sort it's mostly gold or nothing, even if the gold is only silver gilt."

"Well, this is silver," said Mrs. Randall more firmly. "I see it in his room when I'm doing it up."

"Quite sure he's only just got it?"

"He was always saying I shall have to get myself a pencil-and-pen set one of these days. He had a pen, the sort that leaks over the sheets, but he borrowed a pencil off me and never gave it back."

"And you're certain about the initials?"

"Unless it's his crest. I didn't look that close. It was just lying on the table."

"Well, don't show any interest in it, just go on as if everything was all right. We'll think it over."

"Don't wait till she's murdered, too," snapped Grace. The police, say what you like, were just men in uniform, and everyone knew about men. Never do today what you can put off till tomorrow. She was nearly run over on her way to the railway station, so absorbed was she in her own thoughts.

That silver pencil was Len Hunter's undoing; the ironical thing was he had never really wanted it. You couldn't hock a silver pencil and it was a sissyish thing for a chap like himself. But it might come in useful as a present for a girl or something—anyway, there it was and it might be worth a bit and he couldn't bear to leave it and that was the truth. He was feeling very puffed-up, being of those who only live for the hour. He seldom looked back, there was nothing very pleasant to look back on. He was the product of an institution, which had turned him out when he was fifteen to get a living. He had been apprenticed to an engineer, but he had not lasted long there. Youth was coming into its own, lads were getting eight pounds a week painting fences, and anyone with half an eye could get seven. He walked out of the engineering shop within the month and got work at a chain radio store. But they looked rather glumly at his selling a few batteries and a second-hand TV set on the side, so he didn't last long there either. It was the same wherever he went. For one thing he couldn't settle, and for another it was nothing but orders all day. Do this, do that, go there, call at the other place . . . His cards got greasy from being carried around in his pocket. It was a good time to be young in a sense, because the new so-cial services would not let you starve; he looked as old at fifteen as he did three years later, when he went for his National Service, but after a few months they found there was something wrong with his heart and discharged him, and after that he drifted here and there till at last he arrived at Ma Randall's. Not that he meant to stay there long; he was ambitious and he knew that the old one-two at desk or factory never got a man beyond the fifteen pounds a week mark. No

Ford car for him and certainly no lining up for sub-ways and in self-service stores at the end of the day's work. High, wide and handsome, that was how he saw life and how he meant it to be.

He was engaged in a daydream of success when he was brought to his feet by a sound as alarming to him as a revolver shot, though it was merely the tramp of feet on the stairs. Clop-clop, you could no more mis-take those than you could mistake the plod of a cart horse. The police. And coming up to his room. "They've got nothing on me," he told himself val-iantly. "I don't have to be afraid." But under his mask of defiance he was trembling.

Ma Randall's voice sounded outside the door. "You in, Mr. Hunter?"

Well, the old cow knew he was in; even if he didn't answer she'd just open the door. He hadn't had the sense to lock it; anyway she had a master key. He hustled the notes into a drawer before he called out, "Anyone want me?" and opened the door, and there, as he had anticipated, towering behind her, was a cop.

"Can I come in?" asked the fellow in a false bluff voice.

"Can I stop you?"

"Any reason why you should want to?"

"Welcome to my poor abode," Len countered, in his ridiculous dramatic way. "Mind you, I'm not re-sponsible for the furnishings."

"Nothing wrong with the furnishings that I can see," exclaimed Mrs. Randall, huffed at once.

"Oh well," he said, "it all depends on what you're used to."

"And I should like to know what that is," said she wrathfully.

"The best is good enough for me, Ma. Well, come on in if you're coming. I shall catch cold in that draught. Got a delicate chest I have. Had it ever since I was a kid."

The cop nodded to Ma Randall, who beetled off with obvious reluctance. Then he came leisurely in, closing the door behind him.

"What can I do to oblige?" Len drew a flashy cigarette case from his pocket and selected a cigarette, which was a mistake really, because he hadn't a lighter, only a box of matches and the match shook in his hand; you could trust a policeman to notice that.

"Tell you the truth," he said, lounging against the window frame, "I'm used to central heating. Ma's only notion of that is a cup of tea." Languidly he offered the cigarette case.

"Not just now," said the cop, pleasantly. "Been here long?"

"Matter of weeks. I shan't stay, though. Why?"

"We're making inquiries about the death of an old lady who kept a haberdashery—you've heard about it, I daresay."

"Couldn't help it in this house. If she'd been Ma Randall's own sister . . . Heard about it when I got back Saturday."

"Got back? Oh, you've been away."

"Just to the races."

"I see. Have any luck?"

"As if you didn't know. You should have seen Ma's face when I offered her a fiver."

"Going big?" murmured the policeman. All the while he talked his gaze was flickering over the room looking for some hint; his eyes moved quickly like the hovering dragonfly whose movements are so rapid the creature appears almost immobile.

"Backed Mountain Lady." Len flicked some ash onto the floor.

"Ash tray at your elbow," the policeman suggested.

"Good for the carpet. Keep down the moths. Not that they haven't done their worst long ago."

"Mountain Lady, eh? Smart that. Fourteen to one, wasn't she?"

"Twelve to one on the course. You a betting man?"

"I'm married," said the policeman, dryly. "And then people don't give a cop tips."

"Tips nothing. I study form. I know a chap who makes seventy pounds a week betting, all because he knows form. Just choosing a horse because you like the name or the color—that's phooey. You got to *know*."

"Did your knowledge of form help you with the later races?"

"I didn't wait for any other races. Know when to stop. That's nearly as good as knowing what to back. I collected my winnings and came home. I was here by ha'past five. You can ask Ma Randall if you don't believe me."

"You must have put a packet on Mountain Lady."

"My shirt," said Len mechanically.

"And silk at that. Like to tell me something?"

"And if I don't you'll make me? I know."

"You're thinking of some other country," retorted his companion still pleasantly. "The police can't make you do anything here. You could even refuse to answer my questions, though I might think it a bit odd."

"Why? Why should you think it odd, I mean? Do you generally go barging into people's houses and start puttin' 'em through it?"

"I've just told you, you don't have to answer."

"And if you think I know anything about this old girl you're wrong. Why, I never so much as set eyes on her."

"Never dropped into her shop for a pair of suspenders—or nylons for your girl?"

"I don't know what you're talking about," said Len with sudden heat. "I haven't got a girl, and if I had she could buy her own nylons."

"That so? You must be a pushover for them. Quite sure you didn't drop in on Friday? Didn't hear her telling the world she was going to the party and taking all her worldly goods with her?"

Len threw the cigarette on the floor and smudged it out with his toe. "You want to watch yourself," he said angrily. "What the hell d'you think you're getting at?"

"Looking for a little help," explained the sergeant. "That's the way we work. We don't go around find-

ing clues under the carpet and bus tickets in the coal
cellar. That's how they do it in the films but not us.
No, we get our facts from the other chap, the man
who was airing the dog or the old lady running to the
mail box. So, you see, if you'd happened to be in the
doorway and heard Miss Foss telling the world her
plans, you might recall who else was there—get me?"

"No. And I don't want to. And I can't help you
anyway, because I wasn't there. Wouldn't do you any
harm to go out and look for a bit of info for a change,"
he added savagely. "And you can lay off me because I
can't tell you a thing. I've said it before and I'll say it
again if it hasn't penetrated, I never even set eyes on
the old girl."

The sergeant said, "Well, you could have seen her
around, I suppose." He produced a shiny photograph
that he handed over. "Take a peep. You might know
if she had a special buddy or some sort of a Bluebeard
trying to part her from her worldly goods. Oh yes,
that happens in life just as often as in the story books."

Len put out a languid hand and took the photograph. "She had this done for someone's birthday only
a few months back," Creagh volunteered, "so she
won't have changed much."

"Can't think why she bothered," said Len brutally,
handing it back. "Don't we meet enough wet week
ends in this country without framing one and hanging
it on the wall?"

"O.K. Sorry you've been troubled." The policeman
came to his feet; while Len inspected the photograph

he had seen what he wanted. "That's a nice thing," he added casually, as his hand shot out to pick up the silver pencil Len had overlooked, on the rickety table.

"Any objection?" demanded Len, clenching his hands.

"Had it long? Don't mind me asking, do you?"

"Oh—quite a while. Why? D'you fancy it?"

The sergeant turned it sideways. "Got some initials on it," he marveled. "E.F. Not yours, are they? I thought . . ."

"Picked it up second-hand," said Len sharply. "Keeping it till I find a girl called Ethel Ford or—Edith Fotheringay—or . . ."

"Or Emily Foss. How long have you really had it?"

"I told you—weeks. If you're trying to pin this murder on me . . ."

"Only looking for information. I'll take charge of this, if you don't mind. I'll give you a receipt, and . . ."

"Are you suggesting I stole it?"

"Well, it's a funny thing, but we've information that Miss Foss had a pencil just like this—initials and all, and it wasn't found in her bag and it's not among the things at her place."

"Quite a coincidence," said Len, his lips dry. "Who spun you that fairy tale—about the pencil, I mean?"

"Matter of fact, the people who gave it to her. I'm just going to take it along and get it identified. Came from a local shop so they'd have a record, too. By the way, how much did you win on Mountain Lady?"

"About fifty pounds. Nosey, aren't you?"

The policeman whistled. "Must have risked about a fiver?"

"Must have given you a prize for arithmetic when you were at school," Len congratulated him.

"H'm. Care to say where you found it? The fiver, I mean. You hadn't got it Friday afternoon."

"Who says I hadn't?"

"You told Mrs. Randall you had less than a pound. Showed her your wallet, she said."

"You don't want to tell women everything. She'd have skinned me of my last copper, take it from me. I had a hunch Mountain Lady would win and it 'ud be worth putting the lot on her."

"Still, a fiver! They don't hand those out at your sort of job, do they?"

"Oh, it's easier to carry it around in big notes," said Len, pulling out his case, and lighting another cigarette.

"So you had a fiver on you all the time? Suppose Mountain Lady had lost?"

"Well, she didn't, did she?"

The policeman slipped the pencil into his pocket. "Go down alone on Saturday?"

"Matter of fact, I did."

"See anyone you knew on the course?"

Len shook his head.

"Remember the name of the bookie? He'd recall a chap who put five pounds on Mountain Lady, I daresay. Caught the whole betting world short from what I could make out."

"I didn't put the whole lot on with one chap. Got

fried that way before. Shared it out between three or four of 'em."

"Think of everything, don't you?" said the policeman. "Think you'd recognize any of them again?"

"Why should I? Even if I did they wouldn't remember me. Lots of chaps took a flyer on her, I daresay."

"Pity. Happen to mention about the win to anyone? Bar Mrs. Randall, that is?"

"Look here, what sort of a fool do you take me for?"

"I'm not sure yet. Well, that's the lot. Not thinking of moving out in the next twenty-four hours, I take it?"

"What's that to you?"

"Well, I'd want to know where to give you back your pencil, wouldn't I? Wouldn't want to put you to the bother of coming to the station."

"Your initials don't happen to be E.F., I suppose?" Lennie snapped.

"G.C. Bad luck, isn't it? Why, were you going to offer to give it me?"

"When I start giving things to coppers you can sign me up," said the young man, succinctly.

Creagh took out a pen and a bit of paper. "Your receipt," he said. "Well, be seeing you."

After he'd gone Lennie stood staring out of the window, his face nearly black with rage. They'd got him proper. Why the hell hadn't he chucked the pencil away? Funny thing, he hadn't looked at it very clearly, hadn't noticed the initials, and wouldn't have made them out as E.F. most likely if he had—all those silly twisty capitals. He was in a bit of a spot.

"They can't do anything," he told himself several times. "They can't do anything."

But, as so often before, he was wrong.

FIVE

"Yes," said Bessie Marks when Creagh showed her the pencil. "That's the one I told you about, the time you came. Barney had it done at Allports. Emily—Miss Foss—was always saying her points broke—bore too heavy on them, I suppose—so Mr. Marks had this done. Does this mean you know who murdered her?"

"Can't say anything more just for the minute," said the sergeant, civilly. "But, of course, the fellow will have to explain how it came to be in his room."

He had the photograph of Emily that he had shown to Len Hunter, showing a clear set of fingerprints. Creagh never ceased to wonder at the carelessness of criminals; they fell for the same old trick time after time. Within twenty-four hours he knew that Len had been through the hands of the law before today, a case of shoplifting, goods worth two pounds, got off as a first offender. So far as they knew he hadn't broken any more laws, but his record was unimpressive. He reported the position to Inspector Hart.

"That chap, Hunter," he said. "Could be quite an attractive fellow if it wasn't for his expression and his manners. I've been checking up on his record."

"Bad?" asked Hart.

"Well, not what you could call satisfactory. Never

stayed anywhere long enough to put down roots. Not that you can altogether blame him for that."

"Family history?" suggested Hart.

"Wretched. Abandoned as a baby, shoved in an institution, shoved out again at fifteen to get his own living, mother never traced, father unknown. How the hell does anyone expect a kid like that to make good? Makes you sick."

Hart nodded. "Let down all round. Mother, father —daresay he didn't find the institution exactly a home away from home—anything about a girl?"

Sergeant Creagh stroked his smooth-shaven chin. "Well, he fired up at the mention of one. Could be she'd stood him up, too. Another of the crazy mixed-up gang. No actual proof—his story isn't true, but the probabilities are against it. Say he spied the money in the bag, hanging open, saw a chance of easy cash, might have given her a push, not meaning any harm, if you get me—oh yes, it could have happened like that. Of course, if he'd had any sense he wouldn't have gone splashing his money around a few hours later, but if criminals had sense where would we be?"

On the officer's second visit to Mrs. Randall's house he found Len was out, so he said he would wait. Mrs. Randall was talkative enough, but she told him nothing. Never had trouble with him, she said, till this rent business blew up; didn't drink so far as she knew, didn't stay out at night, never tried to sneak a girl in. No complaints from the other lodgers. She startled Creagh by saying, "Misses his mother, I daresay. I know he never really had one, but you can miss them all the same, just like you can miss the leg you were born without."

About half an hour later Len returned. Creagh was waiting for him in the hall. Len shoved his hands in his pockets.

"You again?"

"Waiting for you," the officer agreed. "We'd like you to come along to the station and answer a few questions."

"Still about the old girl? I've told you, I don't know anything about her."

"Not even how her pencil came into your possession? It's been identified. And she was using it not a week ago, so—best come with me."

"If you haven't done anything wrong you've nothing to be frightened about," chipped in Lil.

He laughed, one of those hopeless dramatic laughs of fourth-rate actors. "You really believe that? Maybe I should have a lawyer," he added to the constable.

"You can ring him from the station. Anyone can see you know your rights."

At the station he broke down. "O.K.," he said, "you can have it. I'd have told you right away, but you're always out for the chap who hasn't been lucky. Well, then, it *is* her pencil. Leastways, I never set eyes on it till I saw it in the bag last Friday night."

"Take care what you're saying," Hart warned him. "You can have that lawyer here before you make a statement or answer any questions, only anything you say now . . ."

"I know, I know. I'm not going to confess to the

murder, if that's what you're thinking. I found the bag, see, on a bit of waste ground where the chap that took it had chucked it."

"Yes," said Hart, woodenly. "Remember exactly where it was?"

"Behind that ratty little church. I was walking back about nine o'clock and I saw it chucked down there, a big black leather bag, and I thought it had been thrown out."

"So you picked it up?"

"That's right. Course, I know when fellows make a grab they never keep the bag, just take what's inside it and throw it out."

"Oh, you know that."

"Even kids know that much. I found a bag once when I was about ten; no money in it, of course, just a fountain pen and some keys and a letter. Took it back to the address and the lady gave me half a crown. Said the pen was worth more than that."

"So you thought there might be another fountain pen and you found a pencil instead?"

"That's right. Thought it might come in handy, and nobody wanted it, seeing it had been chucked away."

"Didn't think of bringing it to us?"

"What, a silver pencil?"

"And the rest."

"The rest?"

"The other things in the bag, I mean."

"There wasn't anything else. Well, a shilling or two in a plastic purse."

"No wallet?"

"Nothing in it."

"No? In that case, how did you manage to go to the races next day? Matter of fact, we know she had a five-pound note . . ."

"Trying to trip me, are you? All right, I did find a fiver, folded up small in an inside pocket. Seeing the bag had been chucked out and I wasn't to know who it belonged to, findings keepings, isn't that right?"

"Never heard of stealing by finding?"

"Oh, a diamond ring, say, but—a bag that's been chucked onto a bit of waste land . . ."

"You didn't really think the owner had chucked it there, did you? Why go to all that trouble? Why not put it out with the garbage? And these days not many people throw away a five-pound note, not if they know it's there."

"Then I suppose he didn't."

"Who didn't?"

"The chap who grabbed the bag, of course, the one who bumped the old girl off."

"If you stole a bag, Hunter—mind, I only say if— wouldn't you go through it pretty carefully?"

"I don't suppose I'd think of looking for a five-pound note in a pocket made for stamps."

"But you did, didn't you? That's how you found it. Well, my lad?"

He looked confused, staring furiously from one to the other. "Don't call me that. What are you trying to do? Get me to say I snatched it? Well, I didn't. I found it, like I told you."

"I see, lad. By yourself, I take it?"

His face shut up again, just as it had done that day in Mrs. Randall's house.

"Yes," he said.

The inspector waited a moment.

"I see. Nasty night last Friday, wasn't it?"

"Pretty typical, I'd say."

"Still, hardly the sort of night you'd go walking for pleasure, not when you had a room to go back to, and there were three movies within a stone's throw."

"I was on my way back from the Roxy—took the short cut, see? Want me to tell you the name of the film?"

"Oh, we needn't bother over that. If you went naturally you'd remember, and if you were trying to fox us, well, you wouldn't be such a fool you wouldn't check up. Carry a flashlight by any chance?"

"Why on earth should I? I'm not lame or blind—yet."

"Just wondering how you managed to see the bag in the dark—and the drizzle."

"It had more or less stopped by then. This 'ud be—let's see—about nine, I daresay. There's a lamp on the corner, caught the framework of the bag. Just chance I saw it."

"And that's the fiver you put on Mountain Lady? You didn't think of paying your rent with the money?"

"And have the old girl come at me asking where I'd got it from? She's as curious as a cheese mite, always boring. Besides, I'd been trying to lay hands on a bit of cash all week."

"Didn't think of getting a job?"

"Nothing going in my line. You can ask them at the Exchange," he told them in sudden rage. "Nothing but unskilled labor, and I can't do that. Head, see? Anyway, I got big ideas. I want to be in the money before I'm paralytic."

Hart leaned back. "It's a thin story, Hunter," he said.

The answer came like a flash. "You disprove it, if you can. You've got to make your case, all I do is state the facts."

It didn't help him, all his show of righteous anger and defiance. Within twenty-four hours everyone knew the police had taken a man for the murder of Emily Foss. At best, he had got his times muddled, because according to Mrs. Randall he'd been back well before nine. "Well," Lennie said, "it could have been a bit earlier. Didn't know the police were going to come asking questions or I'd have put the times in my diary," he sneered. Next day they brought him before the magistrate and he was committed for trial.

They found him a lawyer, a little man called Jenks, as unimpressive as his name. He took his client through his story again and again. It was to Len's advantage that he never varied the details. He had won over fifty pounds on Mountain Lady—he stuck to that. No, he couldn't prove it but the police couldn't prove he hadn't—and it was just coincidence that that was approximately the amount missing from Emily's bag. They made inquiries on the race track, but no one remembered him. He had gone down on an excursion with a number of other people, there was nothing special about him. He had come back early because he didn't want to risk losing his gains. He had offered Ma Randall her rent before he knew about Emily Foss's death. The old girl hadn't passed on till the early hours of Saturday morning, and the news hadn't broken before he left the house. Ma Randall happened to mention it in his hearing that same night, but he wasn't apprehensive. Even if anyone had the number of the five-pound note it wouldn't be easy to trace it now. Probably gone through half a dozen hands. He hadn't kept the bag, hadn't kept wallet or purse, and one silver pencil is just like another, isn't it? (He'd never noticed the initials. Well, you wouldn't think anyone would go to that trouble for a plain silver pencil. It 'ud be different if it had been gold.) Anyway, no one had mentioned it and he wasn't planning to hand it on in the near future. He'd gone out on Monday and bought a complete new suit, ready-made of course, though mark you, the day 'ud come when he'd stroll into one of the posh tailors with the best of 'em. Contrary to expectation, he had not gone around to the pub on Saturday evening, just had a meal at a café and come home. No sense trying to cut a swash till you were wearing the sort of clothes that go with it. He knew that everyone suspects a fellow in the money if his getup is shabby. On Monday night they remembered him at the Lone Duck, where he picked up a girl; he had never seen her before and he recognized her almost at once for what she was, a gold-digger, a no-good, the sort that gets you loaded, takes you home and then ransacks your pockets while you're sleeping it off. He had not stayed late, after all, but the manager remembered him because the girl had come back to the bar saying airily she had thought better of it, didn't want anyone singing hymns over her coffin before her time. The policeman traced her, but she could not tell them much, had never set eyes on the chap before, seemed to have a walletful of notes, but not the sort to part easily. Never seemed to have heard of the modern gospel of eat, drink and be merry.

One way and another, there was precious little to help the defense; if Len was guilty this was precisely the story he would have told. Criminals, in the view of the police, generally chose one or two roads: either they tried to rig an alibi, and that was always dangerous, because once you present the police with a lie you have given them something on which to build a case; or they claimed to have gone to the movies alone, and unless something unusual happened like a chap throwing a stone through the screen or a rock-and-roll riot breaking out, it can be hard to show they are not telling the truth. And as it happened, nothing of the kind had occurred at the Roxy that night.

"I don't have to prove anything," Len insisted to his lawyer. "That's their job, and they can't do it—see? So what are you looking like a dying duck for? I could understand it if they felt blue, because they haven't got a case, not without proof . . ." He kept coming back to that.

"They know it all right," Mr. Jenks assured him in

a dreary tone. This case was going to help no one. The jury would be against his client from the start, and Jenks shuddered to think what effect Len would have in the witness stand. He would have kept him out if he could but he knew what the jury would think. "Daren't have him testify," they'd say, and to their confused minds that would be as good as a confession.

"Look," he said wearily, "there's no sense your standing there doing an imitation of a brick wall and saying no to everything. You don't impress me, and you're going to impress the court even less. No jury-man's going to believe you hung about outside the Roxy right up to the time the big film began unless you were waiting for someone. It's not the sort of thing fellows do for fun."

"Call this a free country?" commented Len, deceptively mild. "Never heard it was a crime to stand outside a movie house."

"When the young lady didn't turn up," continued Jenks, as persistent as a coffin worm, "the obvious thing 'ud be to ring up and find out if anything had happened. Wouldn't it?"

"You tell me," Len suggested, "seeing you know all the answers."

"Then it's yes. Now, say you went to this booth and when you got there you hadn't enough coppers. You're wondering what to do, when a lady appears carrying a bag. What could be more natural than to ask her if she could oblige you?"

"And have her scream for the cops?" demanded Len.

79

Mr. Jenks flashed him a hard look. "What makes you say that?"

"Maybe you don't know much about these old girls. Only got to ask 'em the time and they set up a screeching, thinking you're going to rob them of something more precious than life, though how any chap could want to go after such dowdy old skirts . . ."

"If you can't behave youself, Hunter," said Mr. Jenks in a grim voice, "I shall refuse to carry on with the case. Can't you realize I'm trying to save your neck?"

Under the cover of the table at which they sat Len's hands curled and uncurled. The crazy old coot, he was thinking. Can't he see I'm scared blue? How'd he feel in my shoes? Naturally you couldn't say anything to an old guy like this about the nightmares you'd started having—gallows and ropes and white sacks, and last words—but you'd think he might be able to guess that for himself.

But he kept up a front even now. "Thought this was a white man's country," he murmured. "Justice for all, and God defend the innocent. Well, seeing I didn't lay a finger on the old girl, what makes you think I'm within a mile of hanging?"

"I happen to be a lawyer. My job is to do my best for you, and unless you're prepared to coöperate you haven't a dog's chance. A jury might be prepared to consider a verdict of manslaughter if you told them you only wanted change and she lost her head and began to yell and you went to stop her and were a bit rougher than you intended." He thought most likely that was just how it had happened. Len, of course, discerned the weakness of the case at once.

"So I stopped to rob the corpse? That'll make 'em die to save me, won't it? Look here, Mr. Jenks, I know you're doing your best, only so far it's not good enough. There's no girl, so there's no sense looking for her—so far as I recall I'd never been in that phone booth in my life—and I found the bag just the way I said I did. If you want me to learn a story by heart and then commit perjury, just say so, and we'll know where we are. I'm sorry you don't like my story—it's just too bad—but it's the only one I've got, and that's the truth."

From this stance Mr. Jenks was unable to move him.

The police got a small break here, because an enterprising photographer took a snap of Lennie leaving the magistrate's court, and the Roxy doorman happened to see it when he unwrapped a packet of fish and chips shortly before the trial.

"That's the chap," he said and went to the station to turn in his evidence; and that reminded him of the girl who came pelting in twenty minutes after the film started asking about messages. Mind you, there was nothing to tie the two together, but it was an idea. Still, it couldn't help Lennie much, because he'd mooched off, hands in pockets, a good ten minutes before she put in an appearance, and seeing she hadn't come forward or made any application to see the prisoner, it didn't seem likely they were going to identify her.

Len was counting desperately on the fact that no one had traced the diamond brooch to him. The fact of its existence had leaked out; the newsmen had got hold of Sidney Mount and learned the facts before he realized he was talking. The brooch hadn't turned up anywhere. No one had hocked it, and it certainly had not been found in Len's room. Not that that proved anything. It was too hot to touch at present, not valuable enough to be worth the risk of hanging on to. It could have been pushed through the grid of a drain, flushed away, buried somewhere in the country, under a bush, in a ditch. It would need a miracle to find that now.

"Or, of course," said Len painfully, when Mr. Jenks tried to argue the point, "it could be lying cozy in some chap's collar box, some chap who's laughing his fat head off at this very moment, listening to them grilling me and knowing he's safer than most houses are these days."

Mr. Jenks' fears were justified. On trial, during the month of January, Lennie behaved atrociously in the witness stand, lounging against the rail, hands in pockets until told to remove them by the judge, willfully misunderstanding prosecution's questions and being pulled up short again and again.

"The witness must answer the question," the judge decreed.

"He makes it so difficult," drawled Lennie, wondering if they could see his heart pump-pumping inside his jacket. "If he could just put it in plain English—I didn't go to any Oxford or Cambridge myself . . ."

Prosecuting counsel didn't turn a hair. "I will try

and rephrase my question in a form the witness will understand," he said urbanely.

When his turn came counsel for the defense did his best, but he didn't attempt to disguise from himself that his client hadn't much hope of an acquittal, and would be lucky if he didn't get a verdict of willful murder.

When the jury filed out Mr. Jenks watched them mournfully. Half an hour, he gave them, and that mostly for appearances' sake, just time for a cup of tea. He wondered if the boy would be recommended to mercy on the grounds of his youth and the instability of his background, so far as was known; but on the whole he thought not. Young gangsters and hoodlums had aroused a lot of the respectable members of the public, though naturally he would ask for leave to appeal.

He came back just before the half hour was up, but the jury hadn't returned.

He looked around the court, wondering as he had done so often before what it was that made apparently respectable citizens sit for hours in uncomfortable surroundings listening to some wretched creature fighting for his life. It wasn't as though you could find any romantic element here. It was as sordid as could be. A young tough attacking an old woman with fatal consequences. It boiled down to that. All sorts and kinds had turned out to hear the case. He noticed a girl at the back who ought to have been at work, not sitting here in this stuffy court, a pretty girl with fair hair, jammed among three or four elderly gossips. Next to her were two prim housewives. What on earth did they want, neglecting their families? Rag, tag and bobtail, he thought angrily, his eyes scanning the packed benches. All curiosity-mongers, since no one had come forward to speak for the boy, and he had found nobody really concerned with him. It had not proved possible to call his last employers, since he had just walked out. The prosecution had called Mrs. Randall, who had looked miserable enough. . . .

At the end of the second hour the jury asked for advice from the judge, and Mr. Jenks cheered up; it sounded as though it wouldn't go on much longer. Either they would announce their verdict or declare they couldn't agree. Most likely it was one solitary juryman or woman who was holding them up. And this was, in fact, the case, the odd one on this occasion being an elderly spinster of decided views, whose bright grass-green suit clashed with a rimless monocle. An obstinate old so-and-so, thought the foreman, the kind that shouldn't be up for jury service. He shoved his great fist into a silken glove and tried to reason with her.

"Now, Miss Parker, are you telling us you really have doubts as to the prisoner's guilt?"

Miss Parker, who had a mouth like a slide rule, said, "Well, frankly, I think most likely he did do it, though I don't think he meant to kill her. I mean, in that case he only had to catch the ends of her scarf and draw them tight, as that man did in *Blood on the Common;* and he didn't carry a wrench and sneak up behind her like *Blood in the Basement*. (Blood, it should be added, was the name of Miss Parker's pet private eye.) It was unpremeditated, I'd say, because he couldn't know she was going to have all that money on her or be coming into the court just that moment. . . ."

"The judge has explained all that," said the foreman, wearily. "Even if he didn't mean to kill her, he was committing a felony, which not only makes it murder but murder for which a capital sentence can be imposed, even under the new Homicide Act."

"It doesn't make sense to me," remarked Miss Parker. "If he'd just hit her on the head and not snatched the bag he couldn't get more than a life sentence."

The foreman scowled. "It isn't in the least likely he'd have hit her on the head unless he wanted what she'd got in the bag," he pointed out.

"We don't know that he even knew she had more than half a crown," Miss Parker demurred.

She was the difficult kind of juryman.

"Well, we know he took the bag," the foreman snapped.

"We don't even know that," objected Miss Parker. "He says he found it. If that's true all he could be accused of is stealing by finding."

It took them nearly four more hours to wear her down, and it was one of the other jurors who hit on the clinching argument.

"Besides being on the jury here," he said, "we are also citizens, and it's our duty to protect our fellow men and women. Yes, yes, I know Hunter is a fellow man, but you've admitted you think he is probably guilty. In fact, you're really sure of it; it's just a technical point that prevents your throwing in your vote with ours. But say we disagree, or say Hunter is found not proven—which is virtually what it amounts to—what happens? He's as free as air to go out and attack another old woman tomorrow, and it's no use saying this would be a lesson to him, because it's the experience of the police authorities that criminals never learn. They're like kids who can't read. For myself, I'm convinced this boy is a criminal type, and even if you feel sorry for him, though personally I reserve my grief for the poor old lady in the churchyard, you have to admit he's a danger to the community. Murder of this kind with violence is seldom an isolated act. Next time he may try to make certain it doesn't come to a fatal ending, but so long as the intent to make an illicit living off the community exists, and I'm persuaded, we're all persuaded, that's the case here, then you can no more stop this chap from snatching bags, or going on presently to bigger game, than you can stop a canary bird from singing, unless you cut off its head."

He dropped back in his seat, flushed with the effort he had made.

"If silly old characters like Emily Foss will persist in putting temptation in the way of young men like Hunter, they deserve all they get," insisted the old woman, cannily.

The foreman intervened. "That really is a very improper observation, Miss Parker. Our duty is simply to decide if Hunter is guilty. I and ten others of us are convinced that he is and are prepared to say so. Remember, we don't sentence him, that's for the judge. All we are here for is to say whether in our opinion he is guilty or innocent. You have just admitted that you believe in his guilt; for myself, I have in mind all those other unprotected elderly ladies—why, come to that, you could be a victim yourself."

"Ha!" The pigheaded juror let out a screech of laughter. "I'd be sorry for any young man who tried to snatch my bag. He'd be thankful for a National Health Service, I can assure you."

But they wore her down; she couldn't make them see that if he was guilty he wasn't alone in his guilt. The community that had turned him into what he was was equally to blame. And there seemed little doubt that he had, in fact, attacked the silly old girl, though with no intention of polishing her off.

"A recommendation to mercy?" she suggested.

The foreman looked helplessly at his companions. "I really don't think they would accept that. There are no grounds . . ."

So eventually they filed back into their box, the prisoner was brought up, and the astute, the experienced, people in court noticed that none of them looked toward him, so they knew what the verdict was going to be before the foreman answered the Clerk of the Court's question.

Guilty.

The black square was placed on the judge's head. He asked the prisoner the usual question. "Have you anything to say why sentence of death should not be passed upon you?"

"Don't let them see," thought Len, "don't let them guess at the inward terror," because right through the trial he'd convinced himself it couldn't come to this, that this was the one thing too bad to be true. Unfair, rotten unfair. If he'd had a handle to his name or money behind him they'd have got him out of it somehow—that little rat, Jenks . . . He threw up his head and spoke, not to the judge, but to the jury, as he'd been bidden when he took the stand.

"Pity they don't give chaps like me a coffin," he remarked, "or they could use your blankety-blank wooden heads to make it."

That caused a minor sensation. The girl in the back row dropped her head into her hands, and the woman next to her said, "Not going to faint, are you? You shouldn't have come. And think, you wouldn't like a young hooligan like that jumping out on you at night." Though silently she reflected the girl was probably no better than she should be and even might be loitering after dark with no other hope. Len never looked in her direction; it set him up for a minute to see the look of shock that turned the jury into a lot of creased old masks. The judge made no comment, simply spoke the awful words and a minute later he was hustled out of court.

"Well, really," thought Mr. Jenks, pushing through the crowd, "he can't suppose that's the way to do himself any good." He had a word with the defense counsel.

"A wretched case," said the latter. "I'm afraid we only got the verdict I expected. Mind you, we may get a reprieve at the eleventh hour, though how that will improve the situation I couldn't say. Ten to fifteen years in prison isn't likely to turn a young chap like that into a good citizen."

The rest of the court went home to a late tea, and the next day, the very next day, police found the bodies of three alleged wives under the floor of a London lodging house, and the sensation-mongers were after that in full cry. Len Hunter and Emily Foss had vanished like a dream. You wouldn't hear any more of them bar three lines in the press to say that sentence had been carried out—unless, of course, Mr. Thompson was right and there was an eleventh-hour reprieve. Either way Hunter was doomed to obscurity, finished, packed up, put away. That's what they all said.

And "How wrong can you be?" marveled Arthur Crook forty-eight hours later.

He was out to show 'em.

SIX

Mr. Crook was not one of these fussy lawyers who cannot see anyone without an appointment or at least a recommendation. The fact that a man (or woman) was in trouble and thought he might help warmed the cockles of his heart, and he was never put off by appearances.

"Well, in the circus," he would say, looking down at his own nicely rounded figure in its bright brown suit that made sartorial aristocrats shiver, "it wouldn't make sense, would it?"

His clientele was varied to a degree. Men would come in, their pocketbooks bulging, to see if he could find some way of persuading the interfering authorities that at a particular time they hadn't been in some place where about fourteen witnesses claimed to have seen them. If that couldn't be contrived, they would want him to show that even if they were there they were not involved.

"I can't fake evidence," Crook would say, "and if you miss out some of the pieces you can't expect much of a pattern. All I can do is rearrange the bits in a different way from the police and then persuade the old boy on the box (i.e., the judge) that my picture's the right one."

At the other end of the scale were those bumbling

females he lumped together as rum old girls, who presented him with some of the most fetching puzzles that came his way, and who exhibited a forthrightness and independence of thought that enchanted this least servile of men. In between were the flotsam and jetsam who defied analysis.

And a couple of days after Lennie Hunter's death sentence one more of these breezed into the office.

When Bill Parsons, his aid-de-camp, said, "Lady to you," he didn't waste any time asking "Who is she?" and "Has she filled out a form?" He just said, "Show her in," and politely pulled himself to his feet. The girl who flashed past Bill's imperturbable form was as bright as a dragonfly and seemed to move as fast. She was still wearing the jeans and the vivid green sweater that had earned Mr. Jenks' disapproval, topped by a flannel jacket, but Crook saw at a glance that these were clean, and the jauntily tied hair as bright and smooth as the best toffee.

She set her hands—no rings, he noticed, though the color of her nail polish made him think of a slaughterhouse—on the edge of his huge shabby desk, and said, "Mr. Crook, I'm Dinah James. I'm in dreadful trouble and you're the only person who can help me."

"How come you know about me?" asked Crook in cheerful tones.

The girl looked at him in surprise. "Well, London's my home town," she said.

That delighted him. "Rest the feet," he suggested. "Seems it might be a long session, and from the look of you I'd say we had quite a lot of hard work ahead."

Reluctantly she found the chair and hooked it toward her with one foot.

"It's about Lennie Hunter," she said. "You know?"

Crook nodded. "I know. Put on the black cap for him yesterday."

A long shudder passed through her. She might try and play tough, thought Crook, but the reality was as soft as a coddled egg.

"I was there. I expect Lennie was furious, but I couldn't stay away."

"So you're the girl who started everything?" suggested Crook who believed in being direct when people could take it. It was always a comfort when he saw they could. He hadn't been deceived by Lennie's statement any more than Jenks or anyone else.

"Yes." She sounded doubtful. "At least, it wasn't really me, it was the motorcyclist, but from Lennie's point of view it was the same thing. Funny to think a quarter of an hour could make all that difference."

"Meaning he wouldn't wait even that long?"

"Fifteen seconds would be about his limit. You can't blame him really, Mr. Crook, he's been pushed around so much. It's just he's got the idea that people don't think it matters when it's him. It's only Lennie, they say, only Hunter, a chap that doesn't even know his own name."

"That the fact?" asked Mr. Crook, not batting an eyelid.

"Yes. It was like that play they had on TV where the baby's found in a shopping basket at Victoria Station, only in Lennie's case it was Paddington and it wasn't a basket. I don't know if you want all this," she added, hesitating.

"Give me all you've got," said Crook, simply. "How come you know so much?"

"He told me, though I suppose he'd never speak to me again if he knew I'd passed it on, only I must make you understand . . ."

"Why you're for him?"

"Why he didn't do it. He didn't, Mr. Crook, whatever it may look like."

"You didn't give evidence," suggested Crook, drawing his thick red brows together.

"I did wonder, but I didn't see that I could help him; and then him saying over and over there wasn't anyone . . ."

"Like to declare an interest?" suggested Crook. "I mean, engaged or anything?"

"Oh no, Lennie hasn't any time for that sort of thing. And don't get me wrong," she added hurriedly. "There's nothing queer about Lennie."

"Just that he hasn't got any time for anyone but Mr. Hunter?"

"You can't blame him," she repeated defensively. "His mother just handed him over at Paddington like a parcel. 'Oh, do hold Lennie for me for five minutes,' she said to the woman sitting next to her. 'I'm dying for a cup of tea and I'll never get through that jam with a baby.' So the woman took him and said not to be long because her train went in a quarter of an hour, and Lennie's mother disappeared . . ."

"And that's the last anyone saw of her?"

"That's right. In one door and out the other. No one remembered her at the buffet, of course—well, you couldn't expect it. This old girl—Watson her name was, Miss Watson—she saw her train come in and it was an express, but she wouldn't leave Lennie; she tried to find his mother in the refreshment room but of course she'd gone a quarter of an hour before. At last she went to the guard—she lost her train, of course—and they took Lennie to an institution and they called him Hunter, because there was no way of telling what his real name was, and no one ever came to claim him or sent him letters or paid for him—no one belonging to him, that is."

"Anyone else?"

"This Miss Watson. She wrote, and when she heard he was still there she came to see him, and though she couldn't have him, of course, she sort of adopted him, wrote every month and sent him presents and every now and again took him out. That's how I know he wouldn't have killed Miss Foss."

"Because of Miss Watson?"

"He had a thing about old women like that. No, listen. Once we were going to Brighton for the day, sun shining and we'd got the tickets, sandwiches, were going to take a bus on to the Downs. Lennie was like a kid for once. Then just as the train came in some clod banged against an old girl—another Emily Foss, I wouldn't be surprised—and knocked her bag over and all her paper parcels—she was going down to see her daughter and she was hung around like a Christmas tree. This chap never stopped, just pushed onto the train, and the poor old girl was nearly in tears. Lennie and me were aboard but he jumped out and shouted to me to come, too, and he picked up all her things, and shoved them back into the bag, and when she said she felt faint he took her along to have a cup of tea. We missed our train, too, had to go down on a slow one and stood an hour in line for a bus at the other end. Lennie never even cursed. You see what I mean? If it had been one of these madams all swathed in animal skins and flashing diamonds and she'd tried to push him out of the way he might have given her a poke, but he didn't kill Miss Foss, I'm sure of it."

"I might believe you," said Crook, "but thousands wouldn't. How long had you known him?"

"About six months. We met one night in a coffee bar—we were both in London then. Got talking, you know how it is, arranged to go to the pictures next night. Dutch treat, I said, which upset him. He's a funny boy. Course he had a job then, the same as me. Well, we got so we saw a lot of each other."

"Pardon the interruption," murmured Crook, "but did your parents know you were meeting him?"

"My father's dead and I left home soon after my mother married again."

"Not hitting it off with stepdaddy?"

"Some men," said the girl coolly, "don't seem to know the difference between six and sixteen."

"Or know it a darn sight too well. So you upped and fled. Any requests to return?"

She shook her head. "My mother was getting ready for a new baby, and I was nearly seventeen and I suppose she thought I could look after myself. I got into a hostel and found a job—there's plenty of work to be done these days. I wanted to go on the stage, but of course I couldn't afford to go to an Academy, and though I got one or two walk-on parts they didn't lead far, and I didn't know anyone, and you have to eat, so I mostly washed dishes—there's a market for that right around the clock."

"What was Lennie doing?"

"Had a job as a waiter somewhere, but he didn't like it. Then he heard of a job at Burtonwood—at the Porchester—better pay and he was sick of London. So of course I came too. Got a job in Finney's Snack Bar. Not a bad job in summer really, with the tourists— there's an abbey or something somewhere near—I don't know exactly where, I never got around to seeing it—but the buses come to Burtonwood in the holiday season, whatever the weather's like, and of course it being so bad all this summer we were busier than usual.

"He wasn't working at the time of Miss Foss's death, though?"

"No. They didn't treat him right at the Porchester and Lennie said he wasn't any man's black slave. Mind you, they didn't know about his mother giving him away and all that—they'd told him about that at the orphanage—but he always thought they were trying to grind him down. Sensitive you might call him."

Crook thought of a lot more suitable terms, but prudently kept them to himself. "Now, let's get this straight" he said. "You had a date with him that Friday evening?"

"Yes, and there was a bus accident so I missed him. He says he went into the Roxy, and I believe him," she wound up firmly.

"So you said. The times don't fit too well, you know. The big picture at the Roxy wasn't over till nine and on his own showing he must have left by eight-thirty at latest."

"Then I suppose he didn't like the picture. Lennie would never stay where he was bored. He says life's too short."

Crook repressed a mutter. It looked as if it would be short indeed for this unfortunate misfit of civilization.

"I believe everything happened just the way he said," Dinah insisted. "Now you see why I've come to you. I'll do anything you tell me; I did think at first of trying to see him and asking if I couldn't say we both went into the Roxy, but I suppose the police would have found out somehow. He doesn't want me mixed up in this—he hasn't got a lot of use for women —but you're different. I don't know about money," she added abruptly, the color coming into her pale face. "I don't know how it is, I never seem to be able to save anything. I mean, you can only spend your money once, can't you, and it seems safer to spend it now and be sure you get something you want than wait till you're old and past enjoying anything."

"Let's wait till we see results before we talk about money," said Crook.

"I want to be fair," she assured him earnestly. "I mean you must go into this with your eyes open. You —you're not a poor man's lawyer, I suppose?"

"Well, I'm not on the list, if that's what you mean," agreed Crook, "but in another way, you might say I qualified. Now . . ." he handed her a box of cigarettes, but she shook her head.

"I keep thinking. The police are stuck on their explanation, aren't they? They're sure Miss Foss came into the court and someone in the telephone booth saw her and he's the one who killed her. But I don't see that it had to be that way. At least he could have been in the telephone booth but not be a stranger. I read everything in the paper before the trial and I was there at the back of the law court, but nobody ever asked any questions about her. She had a nephew—they didn't even ask if he was in Burtonwood that day, though I suppose he could easily show he wasn't—she must have known a lot of people, mightn't there be something there? Or she could have known something that made her dangerous, and everyone says she had a conscience like a darning needle, long and pricking, and she could have thought it was her duty to pass on whatever she knew."

"You're counting on X's realizing she was going to a party that night though she never did on a Friday," Crook suggested.

"Well, she seems to have told everyone, and anyone who knew her would realize that's the way she'd go. I did think that the money might just be a blind. I mean be taken to make it look like a snatch and grab. Wasn't there a story by Somerset Maugham about a murder in the jungle and everyone thought it was for money because the man was bringing home the wages for the coolies, and ages afterwards they found the money buried under a tree? Well, it could be like that in this case."

"No one can say you aren't a trier," Crook congratulated her.

He didn't laugh, as some men might have done, at the idea of Emily Foss cherishing a secret that might cost her her life. It was his experience that these old women were like Pandora's Box. Spring the lid and jack-in-the-boxes weren't in it. They made all the Victorian melodramas ring true—the missing wills, the abandoned infants who turned out to be heirs to great estates (and a lot of luck that would do them these days), the mysterious voice on the telephone, the dog in the night.

"Lennie know you've come?" he asked.

"No one knows. It wasn't any use till I was sure you'd help."

"Maybe it's just as well he shouldn't, not yet. There's lots of spade work to be done."

"You mean, you will? Oh, I felt certain you'd be on our side, once I'd made you understand about Lennie." It was like a rainbow transfiguring a wet sky. "Can you start right away? There's so little time. Less than three weeks, unless he gets leave to appeal, and he doesn't seem to care."

Crook saw that her face, pale enough when she came in, had turned corpse-white at the thought of how little time there was.

"Never does to trust to chance," he said. "We've got three weeks, less two days. Now, don't look like that. Always remember time's man's slave, not his master," said the heretical Mr. Crook. "When I start giving up to my watch it's time I went on the retired list."

"What can I do?" she pleaded.

"I'll tell you," said Mr. Crook. "Just remember you've put this into the hands of the experts, and get yourself a bit of beauty sleep. You'll want to look your best when the boyfriend comes out, won't you? And remember, too, that the chap who laughs last laughs the longest. Bill and me—that was Bill you saw outside—Bill Parsons, as good a man to have at your back as any I ever met—we're going places right away, and if we don't nominate some other chap for the high jump, I'll—I'll take my retirement pension."

It was the most ardent oath of which he could conceive.

One thing, she wasn't a time waster. Once she'd achieved her objective she stood up, saying, "I must go now. I'm on the afternoon and evening shift, and I didn't say I was coming to London."

She flashed out of the room and down the stairs, running like a young deer to catch her train. She arrived on duty in the nick of time, but it was obvious her mind wasn't on her work. Twice she brought coffee instead of tea (she'd met Lennie at a coffee bar and he told her that first day he couldn't stand tea—sickly

100

stuff, he called it) and the second time the manageress hauled her over the coals.

"If you want to hold this job down you've got to think what you're doing," she said. "That's coffee twice you've brought them instead of tea."

"Oh, what's the difference?" said Dinah, impatiently. "They look the same, they smell and they taste the same, and that's like nothing on earth."

The manageress gasped; Dinah didn't care. She kept thinking about Mr. Crook and wishing she could let Lennie know—only he'd said better not and you could see at a glance he wasn't like that old fool they'd got for Lennie before the trial. Mr. Crook knew how many beans make five and he could make the rest of the world think they were six, if it suited him. That was the sort of man you wanted in a jam like this. Absently she filled a third tea order from the coffee urn.

In the end she compromised by writing to Lennie but not saying anything about her visit of the morning. She didn't know if they'd let him have the letter, or if he'd want it if they did. But it seemed to establish a link, that she needed if he didn't. And she was blown sky-high and almost out of a job a little later for slipping out to catch the last mail, that went at six-thirty.

When Bill looked into Crook's room soon after Dinah's departure he found him sitting hunched like a big ginger owl over his desk.

"We've got a new client, Bill," he said. "That young lady came to ask us to save young Hunter's neck."

"Because he's innocent? Or because he's her man?" asked Bill, in his dispassionate way.

"Well, both. She really does believe in him, and if she didn't she'd have come here just the same. Women slay me," he added frankly. "You'd think that a chap who might, just might have put out another dame's light would be poison to the rest of the sex, but it don't work that way. Look at George Joseph Smith, look at Landru. He only had to put his head around the door and all the dames present fell flat on their faces."

"And not long afterwards fell flat into their graves," agreed Bill, woodenly. "Who does she think did it? Or doesn't she care?"

"Well, of course she doesn't care," said Crook. "Even I know enough about dames to understand that. It's like having your pet dog accused of biting a child. All you care about is having your dog freed. You don't worry about the child. She ain't giving Miss Foss a thought. Now, as I see it, there are only two starters in this race, not like the books written by lady authors where X, having about fourteen enemies who want to see him running in the Churchyard Stakes, makes a point of asking all of 'em down to his country house at the same time, just to make it easier for them to alibi each other. No, either it happened the way the police believe—she was attacked by a bag snatcher who had the bad luck to hit a bit harder than he meant, in which case it's either our man or someone we're never likely to identify—or else Miss F. had an enemy who saw his chance and took it with both hands. That argues premeditation. And that narrows the field considerably. Because X 'ud have to have a motive, and he'd have to know she was goin' to the party. Then he'd know what time she was likely to start, and I daresay it wouldn't be too hard to guess she'd take the short cut. Or it could even be someone who knew she was goin' to telephone that night, in which case she'd be pretty well bound to come by the court. Now if that's the answer, then murder was intended. A local chap or someone she'd recognize wouldn't dare let her give evidence to the authorities, so—the motive wasn't the money in the bag. He could have waited in the phone booth till she appeared and then said, 'Well, I was passing and thought we might have a word, safer than the phone.' Or he could just have followed her when she turned away, seeing the box in use—I don't think she'd hang around on a wet night in her best bib and tucker—and put one hand over her shoulder to stop her mouth and—well, get on with the job. She had the umbrella up, remember. She wouldn't stand an earthly chance. The bag 'ud be a bit of camouflage, to put the police on the wrong track. We'll be able to clear up all those points when we know the chap's name."

"It won't have escaped your notice that it could have been a woman," suggested Bill. "She was no giantress, looked like one of those plucked chickens, and the seven deadly sins flourish as green in little county towns as in the city."

"Yes, that's worth considering," Crook acknowledged. "Fact is, we're in the dark till we know a bit more about the lady. It's a pity she and the nephew weren't on better terms, he might have been able to give us a pointer or two. Or again, he might prefer not to. When a murder's committed," added Mr. Crook, warming to his subject—it 'ud be a furnace soon, Bill realized—"the first suspect is the next of kin. Which brings us to Mr. Mount. Oh, I know he doesn't get a brass farthing from his aunt, but the point is, did he know it?"

"Well, no," Bill agreed. "I hear he's going ahead to contest the will on the ground that the old lady was out of her head."

"He has my sympathy," said Crook heartily. "Any dame who goes out on a wet night, having broadcast to all and sundry that she's taking the contents of the till for a week with her—a week, mark you, Bill—is ripe for the asylum. All the same, murder's murder whether the victim's mad or no."

He reverted to the question of Mr. Mount.

"Now, the truth is we know precious little about this fellow. We know, of course, what he told the authorities, but it could be there's a whole lot he didn't tell them. We know he was in London the day Emily Foss was attacked, and that he'd arranged to pick up his wife about seven-thirty. He seems to have clocked in at the right time—makes you wonder how he could be so sure, don't it? What we don't know yet is whether he had a motive for wanting the old woman underground, though he seems to have cut up pretty rough about the will. I don't want to make myself too conspicuous at the start—I think our man Harries might go down as an advance guard. He's the sort of chap that melts into the landscape and that's the sort we want. He could put out a few feelers, find out if there was any trouble—shop on the rocks, say, domestic rumpus, blackmail even—it could be he was financin' another establishment and didn't want Mrs. M. to know. And wife no. 2 might be makin' trouble."

"Simpler to put *her* light out in that case," suggested Bill, noncommittally.

"Ah, but then he'd be a sitting duck for the police. Someone always comes forward in cases like these to say he or she saw the dear departed with a gent, description given, and sooner or later the police get around to the truth. Might be possible to discover if he's tried touching any of his friends, or seemed to draw in his feelers lately, or had a word with the bank. Yes, I'll get Harries started on that, and in the meantime I'll trundle down to Burtonwood and dig up some of the deceased's buddies. It's wonderful what they'll tell a chap in plain clothes that they wouldn't dream of mentioning to a fellow in uniform."

SEVEN

Crook was not one to let the grass grow under his feet. He contrived to obtain copies of all the documents in the possession of the police, read all the newspaper reports—"Always read the local rags," he told Bill. "They give you that little bit extra that sometimes helps you to spot your man. . . ." And he had demanded an interview with a shocked and incredulous Mr. Jenks. Mr. Jenks let it be seen that he considered Crook's behavior in intervening at the eleventh hour both reprehensible and professionally unsound.

"My client," he began, but Crook interrupted him, saying robustly, "But he ain't your client any more. You've given him the bird—or rather, you've delivered him up to the executioner. I'm his last hope."

When he had collected every available jot of evidence, in addition to some information not available to the police, Crook went through it all with a fine tooth comb.

"Mount's telling the truth about being in London that day," he assured Bill. "Harries has been on the trail and tracked him to Copes, where they had one of their silver auctions. He bought a couple of things, nothing very fancy, and paid by check. He's known there, though he doesn't spend much. No one particularly noticed when he left, but he happened to remark to the police that he was a bit late picking up Mrs. M. because of the accident to the bus at this end. Now, I've seen all the local papers, but the only reported accident is the one in which Dinah James was involved, so it seems probable he traveled to Burtonwood on the same bus."

"In another minute," suggested Bill, "you'll be telling me she noticed him."

"I don't think, in the state she was in, she noticed anyone. She was only worried about what was going to happen if she turned up late. Even if she thought she did, you know as well as me no court would accept that as evidence. It's not as if they'd ever met before. She didn't even know Miss Foss's nephew kept a jeweler's shop, probably didn't even know she had a nephew. Still, if he was on that bus, how come he reached Elsham so late? He picked up Mrs. Mount at seven-thirty—everyone's agreed about that—but the bus—he'd get it at Finney's Bridge, where he had to change in any case—arrived in Elsham at seven P.M. It was due at six-fifty but, as we know, it got held up. It managed to recover ten minutes on the way. It wouldn't take him above five minutes to reach Baynes Crescent where Mrs. M. was spending the evening, but he doesn't arrive till seven-thirty."

"Went back to the shop?" offered Bill.

"He doesn't say so. Anyway, why should he? But— say he left the bus at Burtonwood at six-five. It's quite a piece to Love Street—ten minutes say . . ."

"So he'd arrive at six-fifteen. He ought to have caught his aunt then."

"Yes. Though he could argue he must have missed her by a couple of minutes. You have to remember it was foggy and drizzling, and he hadn't gone that way by bus for quite a while. Or, of course, he needn't have gone to the house at all, but have made straight for the court."

"Knowing she was going to telephone?"

"It could be. She hadn't a phone in the house, and this was the nearest. 'Ring me on Friday night,' he could have said . . ."

"Knowing she'd be going to the party?"

"He says he didn't know, but that's what you'd expect. He may simply have taken for granted that she would take the short cut. Or—most likely—he could have watched her go out and followed her. Not much likelihood of being seen on such a night, and a cinch that no persons who saw him would recognize him. Anyway they did not see him, or if they did they've their own reasons for not coming forward. I'll make the rounds, by the way, in case there is anything to pick up that the police have overlooked. It was doubtful odds against anyone hanging around in the Court; if there had been anyone he'd have had to have changed his plan or waited till X had departed. Of course, if we could show he knew about the party being that night it 'ud help, but the only way to prove that is to get the fellow to trip himself up."

"Motive?" murmured Bill, whose job was to pose all the questions the opposition would ask.

"That's a thing we'll have to find out. The police are luckier than us, they don't have to show one. In his case, it ain't likely to be anything but cash. It strikes me, Bill, the time's come for me to leave you to hold the fort this end—I'll give you a number where you can get me the other end as soon as I arrive—while I go down to Burtonwood. I'll put up at the local inn if they can take me and scout around for twenty-four hours before I move on to Elsham."

The Seven Moons was about half full when a big forceful fellow came marching in in a bright brown suit, and with red hair and eyebrows that bristled like the quills of the fretful porcupine. He leaned on the bar and ordered a pint. This he consumed at a single swallow and pushed the tankard back across the counter. After this there was no difficulty in getting into conversation with the landlord. Crook said things were a bit quiet, weren't they?

"It's early yet," said the landlord, whose name was Pigott. "Things brisk up a bit later in the evening. Not that business is what it was, not with all this TV about. Lots of chaps who used to spend the evening here just come in, have a pint and out they go; the most they do is take a bottle home, but it's not the same thing."

"Still, there are the chaps who can't abide TV who'd be driven here on that account," Crook tried to console him. "Chaps who'd never have come in the days of good old radio."

"Well, it's the women," Mr. Pigott confessed. "They like to think the family all gets together of an evening, put their feet up on a TV stool, wearing TV slippers, eating their tea off a TV plate, and park their beer on a TV table. And when they do come in all they talk about is what they saw on TV last night and if it was better than the B.B.C. So far's I can make out," he added grumpily, "it's always a murder play of some sort, so what's the odds?"

"Well, they don't have to turn a switch to get that," commented Mr. Crook, jumping in as neatly as a ball player taking a catch. "Had one yourselves in these parts pretty recently, didn't you?"

"Miss Foss? Well, but the police have buttoned that up," objected Mr. Pigott. "What they like's a bit of mystery."

"Maybe they'll get that thrown in in this case, too. After all, what's been buttoned can be unbuttoned if you get a chap who knows the ropes."

Mr. Pigott looked startled. "Meaning the chap's going to appeal? I thought . . ."

"Don't see what grounds they could offer," conceded Mr. Crook. "No, it 'ud mean starting from scratch. After all, the police jumped on the fellow most likely to be guilty. For them there wasn't anyone else in the picture. But supposing there was another chap who slunk out before the police appeared on the scene?"

Mr. Pigott showed signs of excitement. "You the young chap's uncle?" he asked.

"Lennie Hunter's Uncle Arthur? Well, you might put it that way. Didn't know the lady yourself, I take it? I mean, she wasn't one of your regulars or anything?"

"Good thing she can't hear you," said Mr. Pigott.

"Die of a heart attack, she would, if she hadn't died already. Why, I don't suppose she ever had a bottle of anything stronger than milk in the house since the old man died."

"That so?" Mr. Crook's red eyebrows shot up. "Dad tipple, perhaps?"

"Not that I ever heard. Gone ninety when he died, you know, and not much with us, as you might say, during those last three years. Had brandy around for medicinal purposes . . ."

"That all? It's enough to turn a chap into a chronic invalid. Not that brandy 'ud be my cup of tea. Still, since he left us for a more peaceful world, she might have spread her wings a bit."

But Mr. Pigott said firmly he could put that idea out of his head. "For one thing, she didn't hold with drink. Never set foot over this threshold, not even in a friendly sort of way at Christmas or anything like that. Not one of these solitary boozers either," he said. "You know, the kind that sops up alcohol mixtures when nothing else is handy. For another, she was pretty close with her money. Never spent a ha'penny if there was anyone else to spend it for her. No, the church was her pub. A good time here and a reward in the world to come."

"A good time? Come now . . ."

"It was what she wanted. You should have seen that crowd chatter when they met on a corner—out of shop hours, of course. The United Nations hadn't anything on 'em. Seems odd to think of her getting murdered. You'd have said if there was a woman living who'd die in her bed with the parson doing his stuff over her, it 'ud be Emily Foss."

"This young chap they've taken for it," persisted Mr. Crook, adding, "Same again and have one yourself. Ever see him here?"

"I wouldn't say he never came in, but not to notice. We get a good crowd Friday and Saturday, and he could have had his pint with the rest. But I don't recall him. The coffee bar on the High Street is more his line. Sit there yapping half the night, these young chaps do. With their girls, of course."

"He said he didn't have a girl," said Mr. Crook, carefully.

"A chap dressed to kill the way he was when they picked him up isn't the type to go around solo," observed the landlord sagaciously. "Besides, who was he waiting for outside the theatre?"

"Little Sir Galahad?" suggested Mr. Crook. "I am content to walk in the shadow so long as the sunlight falls on you . . ."

"Well, it could be that way. Or he might have thought he could play the hand better if his partner was dummy. It's true no girl ever came forward, but you can hardly blame her for that. It wouldn't do her any good to have it known she went around with a murderer."

"He's not swung yet," Mr. Crook reminded him, rather severely.

The door was pushed open and another customer came in. "Here's the gentleman you want," said Pigott. "Evening, Mr. Bastable. The usual?"

"That's right, George." The newcomer saw Crook and nodded cheerfully.

"This gentleman's down from London about Miss Foss," Pigott offered.

"A relative?" Bastable looked surprised. "You're not the nephew, are you? I thought he . . ."

"No relative," said Crook hurriedly, lugging a card out of his pocket. "Crook's the name, Arthur Crook, and I'm here in young Hunter's interest."

"Hunter? That's the chap who did it."

"The chap the police have picked," returned Mr. Crook firmly.

"And you don't think that's the same thing?"

"Could be," allowed Mr. Crook. "But I can't see they actually proved their case."

"Well, I suppose a chap doesn't commit a murder in the presence of witnesses, not unless he's mad," suggested Bastable.

"Most murderers are mad," conceded Crook. "Mad to think they can pull a fast one not only on the police, but even on the whole community."

Bastable was looking puzzled. "Mean you've got a notion it was someone else?"

"Meaning it could have been. Anyway, if I can get my client the benefit of the doubt it 'ud get him off the rope. I take it you knew the dear departed."

"I don't know anything about her I didn't pass on to the police, though," Bastable assured him.

"We-ell, I wonder. No, I ain't doubting your word, only my guess 'ud be you answered their questions."

"Well?"

"You could have known something more that they didn't ask you about."

"Such as?"

"Well, I don't know yet," confessed Crook, handsomely. "What are you having? No, my turn, if you'll permit me. Same again for me, George, and if you've five minutes to spare—this was to Bastable—I'd be mightily obliged."

They carried their drinks over to a table. "I gathered from my client that Miss Foss confided quite a bit in you," he offered, invitingly.

"I wouldn't exactly say confided was the word. She'd tell you what she wanted you to know, but you'd need a corkscrew to get anything else out of her."

"When you heard she'd been attacked how did you feel? Astonished?"

"Barney seemed to take it for granted it was a bag snatcher. I was shocked and—well, I suppose you could say surprised, as you would be about anyone you knew who'd come to grief, but when I heard she'd got all that money on her, well, it seemed to me asking for trouble."

"She wasn't supposed to know there was going to be a snatcher in the alley, court, whatever it was."

"No. But there's generally trouble of some kind at Harton Races; chaps come down from London and in from the outlying districts, to say nothing of our own fair share of crooks and hoodlums. What beats me," he added reflectively, "is why she broadcast it to everyone that she'd be carrying the stuff. I mean, half the place seemed to know."

"I heard she had a thing about burglars; I reckon she thought that if it was known she'd have the money on her, no one 'ud bother to break in."

"I suppose that could be it. What makes you think it wasn't young Hunter?"

"I never said it wasn't. I only said there's no cast-iron proof that it was. Of course, it could have been another bag snatcher, but there's also the chance that it was a personal affair."

"You mean, willful murder? Emily Foss?" Bastable sounded staggered. "You never knew her, of course?"

"No. But I've yet to learn there's any sort of person who's immune from murder."

"Ah, but you're suggesting a premeditated crime. You need an enemy for that."

"And I've yet to learn there's anyone living who don't have an enemy. From what I can learn, you saw quite a lot of the lady, used to ring you up and consult with you . . ."

"About the church," said Bastable. "Oh yes, she was always going on about that. Why can't we start rebuilding? Why isn't there enough money? Let's have a special collection. We'd had two or three already. You can't go on getting blood out of stones, but you couldn't make Emily see that."

"You didn't know her in a private capacity?" Crook hazarded.

"She didn't think much of my legal ability," Bastable

confessed in rueful tones. "Mind you, I didn't draw up her will or anything like that, but she did consult me now and again, semiprofessionally, if you know what I mean."

"I know," agreed Crook. "Stop you in the street or after church and ask your advice, but not come to your office where you could send a bill."

Bastable looked amused. "You seem to know all about it."

"Lawyer myself," murmured Crook.

Bastable looked startled. "Yes, of course. I'd forgotten. Well, there was a question about the lease of the premises. She had the shop on a long-term lease, and it was coming to its completion. Miss Foss wanted to renew, but of course property's increased in value since her father signed the last lease twenty-one years ago, and she thought it monstrous that her rent should go up. No sense pointing out to her that the place was worth more now than it used to be. 'If it's worth more it's because I've built up the business,' she'd say. Same with income tax. 'Why should the Government make these heavy demands?' she asked me. 'I've done all the work, earned the money, haven't I?' "

"You'll never make dames see eye to eye with the authorities about money," Crook acknowledged. "Mind you they're logical in their way. 'It's my money, why shouldn't I have the spending of it? To say nothing of the fact that I should lay it out much less wastefully than they would.' And they may have something there, you know, Bastable."

"Well, don't we all know we could do better than

the Government?" Bastable grinned back. "There was another thing. She thought of money as—well, like a bird in a cage. Put it inside, shut the door and let it sing till you're ready to take it out again. I remember her investing some potty little sum once, about a hundred pounds, and then something happened and the shares fell, and you'd have thought it was the sack of Rome. Gave her a permanent jaundiced eye on every kind of investment—except Government bonds, of course, and we all know what they're worth at the present time. And when she set her heart on a thing, like this church rebuilding, a tank wouldn't budge her. I've often thought it was lucky for some chap she never set out for a wedding ring. He wouldn't have stood a chance."

"According to some of the pubs," remarked Crook, "she'd actually got someone in her eye."

"Don't you believe it," said Bastable. "If anyone had known about that, I would. No, she was like an old aunt of mine, thought it would be indelicate to care for a gentleman."

"About this announcement she was going to make," urged Crook. "You think it had to do with the church fund?"

"I'm as sure as anyone can be without actual proof. She'd got a—what's the word?—a phobia about it. Always fretting in case labor costs went up, and our bills with them. 'Why can't we get started right now?' she'd say. 'Once we've got a signed contract they can't go back on their word.' I quoted the text about the man going forth to make war making certain his army wouldn't be annihilated in the first battle. No sense pulling down the present building and then finding ourselves worshipping in a place without a roof. Patience, I told her. After all, the money's earning a nice bit of interest while we're waiting. That was a mistake. I shouldn't have mentioned the interest. It set a fresh bee buzzing in her bonnet. Was I sure the brokers were honest? She'd heard of firms using their clients' capital and then when it was wanted it wasn't there. Honestly, Crook, I was sorry for the old girl, but she nearly drove me nuts. If you're in doubt, why don't you get in touch with Jones and Allen and ask for yourself? I said. Only it's no use coming to me and asking me to act for you if you find yourself involved in a libel case. That calmed her down a bit, though between ourselves I'd never have been surprised if she had gone up to London. Only of course she wouldn't desert the shop, and on Sundays there was the church. It wouldn't surprise me," he added, "if they find bags of notes hidden under the floor at her place. Honestly, she was a monomaniac where money was concerned."

"Anyone thought of looking?" asked Crook, his lively imagination instantly captivated at the thought of the old woman lifting boards (probably by candlelight) and stealthily depositing her gains where neither bank nor broker could pillage them.

Bastable grinned. "Maybe we should give the authorities a hint," he said.

"Good idea," acknowledged Crook, solemnly. "By the way, ever meet the nephew?"

"No. And I don't think she did, oftener than

she could help. I gather," he added cautiously, "he was in a bit of a spot at one time. No, she didn't actually say so in so many words, but she was very indignant about people taking it for granted they could call on you in emergencies that had no right to arise. I don't think he ever came to Burtonwood, not within my knowledge. She didn't like the wife for some reason. Well, that often happens."

"She never dropped a hint that *she* might be in difficulties?" Crook insinuated.

"What sort of difficulties? Financial? Oh, I shouldn't think so. She was very wary about money, was Emily. Of course she never spent any. There is one thing," he added, "though I don't know whether it has any bearing. She was going to make some sort of announcement at the meeting that Saturday, the day after she died. She kept after me to say it was important that all the committee should be present. I know she drummed up several of the others in person. She didn't say what it was going to be, but my own impression was that she was going to make a generous gesture and donate enough to make it possible to get the work started. Or she may have been going to say that she'd contribute something handsome if five others would do the same. Something like that."

"Do you remember exactly what she said?"

Bastable considered. "The police asked me about that, but you know how difficult it is to remember exact phrases. Something like, I'm not satisfied with this dillydallying about an important work. I believe I can persuade the committee to take steps. And something about not minding what it cost her or words to that effect. If you're trying to tie this up with her death," he added, "I don't see the connection myself."

"Nor do I," Crook acknowledged. "Not yet. One more thing. You don't think she could have been involved in something—well, shady?"

"Emily Foss?" Bastable's tone answered the question, but Crook refused to be silenced.

"It happens to the least likely people. There could be something years back, something she never spoke of—I mean, no one was bleeding her? Or . . ."

"What are you driving at?" demanded Bastable. "Surely not blackmail? You can forget the idea. She wasn't the type."

"There isn't a type," said Mr. Crook, unemphatically. "People get a notion that you have to be a—a roisterer or a woman of the world to get into the clutches of a blackmailer, but it don't work out like that. I remember some years ago a case in which I was interested. There was an elderly woman concerned, a devout creature, very quiet, sacrificed her youth looking after an aged father, rather like the lady in this case. She lived in a small town, kept herself to herself, then one day she tried to commit suicide, and the facts came out. It seems that her papa had died a bit suddenly, but no one thought much of it. He'd been ailing on and off quite a while, there was a nurse on the premises at one time; then he died one night in his sleep. The doctor wasn't particularly surprised. The old chap was touching eighty; he sent up the certificate, there was a bang-up funeral and the daughter set up house for herself.

What nobody knew for nearly five years was that she'd doped Papa's medicine after she learned he was proposing to marry again and cut her out of the will. Mind you, she thought she was safe. Nobody else knew—except the nurse. The old gentleman had confided in her, and she got suspicious. She pointed out to Belinda Slapcabbage that she didn't want any trouble, only she wasn't as young as she had been and a nice steady income without working was what she was after. She'd been bleeding Belinda white for years, perpetually putting up her price, till she overplayed her hand."

"And you think Miss Foss may have hustled the old gentleman into a better world? Well, all I can say is I never heard a whisper of anything like that. Mind you, it's true I wasn't living in Burtonwood at the time. I didn't come till '45. I was in London until then. In '44 a V.1. got our flat, reduced the place to rubble. You never saw such a shambles. We lived in a square and the damn thing came down in the middle of it, and the blast couldn't get out, just went round and round like a mouse in a cage. I wasn't at home at the time, and when I did get there I tell you I couldn't identify my own house at first. Mrs. Bastable was in and—they said she wouldn't have known anything about it, probably knocked out by the blast in a second, only you can never be sure, can you? It was three days before they dug down to her." He fell abruptly silent.

"I remember the V.1.s," acknowledged Crook. "Shook up the folk as nothing else had done since the outbreak of war. Funny thing, they looked like kids'

toys when you saw them gleaming silver in the sun.
First time I saw the result of an explosion, up in Church
Street, Kensington way, my eyes nearly dropped
out. . . . Anyone here who would remember the old
gentleman?" he added.

"Oh, plenty I should imagine. But if you think she
was being dunned I fancy you're barking up the wrong
tree. At least, there was never a suggestion that she'd
been drawing large sums or paying out checks, not that
I heard anyway. And in any case," his forehead wrin-
kled, "if that was so, why should she be attacked? If
she'd been doing the blackmailing, that 'ud be a different matter. But you can't imagine Emily . . ."

"She might have got to know something . . . Still,
as you say, that's a long shot. Any notion who were
her special buddies?"

"Church folk for the most part. You live in London,
so it's hard to realize that democracy's still a word in
these little country places. You know the crowd on
your own social level, but not the one above or the one
below. That is, you know the village, or you know
the county. Emily knew the village. To do her justice,
I don't think she wanted to know anyone else. I can
give you two or three names, but I fancy the police
went around pretty thoroughly when they were here."

"There's another thing," Crook continued. "It took
the jury nearly six hours to reach their conclusion, so
someone had doubts."

"That was Miss Parker. But I wouldn't put too much
reliance on that. She didn't like the foreman—well,
he does throw his weight about a bit, and she wouldn't

mind thwarting him. Still, they won her over in the end. Best thing for Hunter that they did," he continued thoughtfully. "If they'd failed to agree, what would have happened? Another trial, and that one would probably have brought Hunter in guilty same as this one did. Simply prolonged the agony. Still, I don't see there'd be any harm your having a word with Miss Parker if you feel like it. She might be able to tell you quite a bit about the old man. Not that she and Miss Foss were on any but the most formal terms. Her father was the last rector but two, she never went near the church, but she's spent all her life here. A gardening type," he added. "Calls a spade a spade when she doesn't call it something more indelicate. And of course," he added, "there's always the nephew. He's fighting the will, though speaking as a lawyer I don't think he has much hope. Still, that's one thing about the law. You never can be quite sure which way the cat will jump."

They had another round, this time at Bastable's expense, and chewed the fat about the deceased; Bastable repeated what he had already told the authorities and Barney Marks. "There's a chap you might go and see," he added. "It was Marks who found her. Bessie Marks probably knew Emily as well as anyone. She was a good friend to her when the old man was alive according to all accounts, when she (meaning Miss Foss) was pretty well tied down by his demands and the shop. Not that I anticipate you'll learn anything fresh, but you might be able to draw different deductions from it."

Crook grinned and thanked him and said he wouldn't be a bit surprised, and then Bastable went home to the tasty meal Kate Winter, his housekeeper, had prepared for him, and Crook took a hand at darts with the usual results. George Pigott could fix him up with a bed for as long as he wanted it, and thither he repaired in good time. On the whole, he reflected, it hadn't been at all a bad day.

EIGHT

Next morning he was up bright and early and set out on a round of visits. He'd be here a while, he shouldn't wonder, and they might as well get used to the sight of him. It was a cheerful frosty morning, and he wasn't surprised to find Miss Parker already at her hobby of working in the garden. Seeing the fantastic car pause at the gate she sat back on her heels and shouted, "If it's about the election, we vote conservative here."

"Jake by me," said Mr. Crook, politely, climbing down and coming to the gate. "Mr. Bastable mentioned your name. And I didn't know there was an election. And if I had known I wouldn't have been interested, not being a native."

Miss Parker threw down her fork and came amply to her feet. She had what Crook called a gardening face, open-featured, shrewd, weather-beaten and (he would have sworn) undefeatable. He reminded himself it had taken her fellow jurors nearly six hours to wear her down.

"Don't tell me there's anyone left who minds his own business?" she said in incredulous tones.

"If I poke my finger into another fellow's pie it's because I'm being paid to do it," said Mr. Crook, beaming.

"Anyone paying you to come down and stop me

thinning out the weeds? Seeing nobody likes them you'd wonder they come crowding in the way they do. They're like some people, no shame."

"Understand you were connected with the Hunter affair," insinuated Crook.

"That poor devil! I thought that was settled."

"No question is ever settled until it is settled right," declaimed Mr. Crook, breaking suddenly into quotation. "Tell me, one chap to another, what made you think he might not have done it?"

"Who says I thought that? Because it's not true. Everything points to its being him and most likely it was, but I don't think it was murder. These wacky old girls advertising all around the neighborhood that they'll be going out after dark carrying all their savings are simply asking for it. And if he did it I don't believe he meant to. Just a case of plain grab that turned out wrong. Manslaughter perhaps—but the jury wouldn't have any of that. If I thought he was the one that did it, then it was murder, that's the law, they said."

Crook nodded. "That's O.K."

"Ever since the sentence I've been bothered. Suppose, just suppose, we were wrong? I don't sleep as well as I like and during the night when they tell you that resistance is at its lowest, I try and think how I'd feel in his shoes. Convicted of something I hadn't done and knowing I couldn't prove it. How do you prove you're innocent when appearances are against you and you haven't got an alibi?"

"Get the right lawyer," said Mr. Crook succinctly.

"That poor devil," repeated the woman. "Not a friend in the world to care if he swings or not . . ."

"That's where you're wrong. Even if he didn't have anyone before, and I'm not saying he didn't, he's got me now. Even though he don't know it," he added.

"And you think you can prove he didn't do it? In the teeth of the evidence? And the judge's summing up?"

"Only one way to do that, what you might call the indirect way. I can't show he wasn't there, I don't see how anyone could. But if I can show someone else was . . ."

"And you think you can?"

"Well, that's my job," said Crook, looking a little surprised.

"And you think I can help? Well, you don't look the sort of fellow to waste time just for the fun of it." Miss Parker could be as direct on occasion as Crook himself. "If you've got some idea that I know anything . . ."

"Not about Hunter. You might know something about Miss Foss."

"You'd better come in," said Miss Parker, opening the gate and untying a hefty Hessian apron patched with pockets. She led the way into the cottage. "Emily Foss? She and I weren't on intimate terms, y'know."

"Still you knew her, maybe you acknowledged a word or two now and again. You'd both lived here all your lives, according to local report . . ."

"Too true." Miss Parker heaved a gusty sigh. "I've always been meaning to get out and about for a while,

127

and then I think, how do I know I'll like any place better than this? And—here I am."

"Same here," beamed Crook. "Paris, Rome, New York? What have they got that London hasn't got? You can keep it. Now, it could be someone wasn't too sorry to know that the angels in heaven are singing today, 'Here's Emmy, here's Emmy, here's Emmy.'"

Miss Parker looked dubious. "Never heard of her having any enemies, not to the pitch of risking murder," she said. "Anyhow, they wouldn't hit her over the head in a dark corner. More likely ask her to tea and put a pinch of arsenic in the scones, like that lawyer chap . . ."

"Awfully difficult to do the job that way and not find the limelight shining dead on you," Crook warned her. "Besides, you might get the wrong scone yourself. Accidents will happen. Ever hear her say anything that 'ud give you a lead?"

Miss Parker shook her head. "Kept herself to herself. Never went visiting or asked people in, apart from the church bunch. Efficient woman," she added abruptly. "That shop was in a bit of a pickle when the old man went. He'd been more than a bit *non compos* during the last year he was in charge, but Emily took over and got everything straightened up. Wouldn't be surprised to know she turned a pretty penny, and goodness knows she never parted without a major operation. If there'd been a fancy dress ball here she could have gone as a scarecrow just by walking out of the shop. Neat and all that, but she looked as if she'd robbed a jumble sale. And it wasn't that she couldn't afford something better. I remember not long ago the shop next door became vacant. I happened to be matching up some ribbon when someone said, 'I wonder you don't take it over. You could do with a bit more space.' And she looked up like a little offended marmoset and snapped, 'When I have four hands and four feet I'll think about it. At present I've got as much as I can manage here.' This woman—I don't know who she was—said, 'Well, but couldn't you put in a manager?' And she said, 'When you've got the reins in your own hands you can take the carriage which way you like. Hand 'em over and you may be heading straight for bankruptcy within twelve months. And who's going to pull me out then? I haven't any rich relatives—quite the contrary.' Her voice was like—oh, like the sting of a wasp. Dig. Dig. I remember thinking, Who was that meant for? This other creature, who seemed to have more leisure than sense, said, 'Oh well, the bank would always give you a hand,' and she said, 'I don't hold with borrowing any more than I hold with lending. Once the money's out of your pocket and in someone else's you've no guarantee it'll ever come back. That's good sense, isn't it?' "

"Logic anyway," Crook agreed.

" 'It's a pity everyone can't see it,' Emily Foss went on. 'To hear some people talk you'd think money grew on trees. I work very hard for what I have, and I don't work to keep other people in luxury.' I remem-

ber thinking, Well, you've got your knife into someone pretty deep. Mind you, I did wonder who had the
nerve to try and part Emily from her brass."

"H'm," said Crook, thoughtfully. "No harm guess-
ing. How long ago was this?"

"I won't swear to chapter and verse, mark you, but
some time this summer."

"Might be pretty significant," admitted Crook. "Any
notion what she'd call luxury?"

"Your car, my summer holiday, a canary in a gilt
cage, an armchair for spare time. Mind you, she had
the shop painted—that was business, but I believe she
hasn't had a room done over on her own premises
since the old man died."

"But not so mean when it came to the House of the
Lord," suggested Crook.

"Oh, I'm not saying Emily didn't have her good
points," conceded Miss Parker, "but then so has a
hedgehog, and no one would want to take that for a
bosom companion."

"Never heard tell of a viper?" murmured Crook.

"What? In Emily Foss's bosom?" Miss Parker
seemed to consider making a crack, but thought better
of it. "It 'ud have to be a mighty small viper," she con-
tented herself with saying. "Do you know she had a
nephew, but she never took any notice of him? That's
not gossip, anybody would tell you the same. Well,
even if you don't care much for your nephew, you
generally don't take it out on the child. Especially at
Christmas. Me, I always ask for something for the garden. That gives plenty of scope. But Emily Foss 'ud

have thought twice before sparing a weed. Might have come in useful making a grass skirt for one of the happy heathens her persuasion supported. No, I can't see what anyone, bar a bag snatcher, stood to gain from her death."

"Except the church," offered Crook.

"I'm like the White Queen," acknowledged Miss Parker. "I can believe in six impossible things before breakfast, but that one of the church gang would lurk with a hatchet and hit her over the head, no, that's the seventh. Sorry I can't help you," she added, quite genuinely.

"Lady, you may have told me a lot more than you know. I've got a nice picture of Miss Foss in my mind."

"I daresay you lump us all together, old witches waiting in line for our broomsticks and black cats," offered Miss Parker, bluffly.

But Crook said, what was wrong with witches anyway? He'd known some classy specimens himself, and retrieving his vividly checked cap, that he had stuffed into his pocket, he took himself off.

Leaving Miss Parker, he trundled himself around to the Marks house.

"It's a funny thing," said Bessie Marks when she had heard what he wanted to know, "but Barney has said more than once that he wouldn't be surprised to find there was some secret in Emily's past."

"Any evidence," asked Crook, "or just good old feminine intuition functioning for once?"

"I think it was chiefly that he couldn't believe anyone's life could be quite so grim as hers was. Mind you,

131

he's wrong. Lots of women in her generation had just the same sort of experience. Of course, there's no knowing how things would have turned out in different circumstances, but she always gave me the impression of being the spinster type."

"I suppose your husband never made any suggestions as to what the secret might be?"

"I don't think he had any ideas. Mind you, if the police are right and she was killed for her money, the odds are that there wasn't a secret."

"Too true. Still, it's stretching the imagination a bit far to suppose anyone would take the chance of knocking off an old dame like that for the sake of what her bag might contain. And if it was someone who knew, well, that 'ud argue a customer or an acquaintance anyhow, and that don't seem very likely either."

"Barney's mulled it over and over," admitted Bessie, "and we can't think of any reason. You can't suppose she knew anybody's dark secret, and only the church profited?" She laughed. "Oh dear, I suppose it isn't funny, but you can't suppose the pastor would strangle her. . . ."

"I didn't know she was strangled," said Crook sharply. "I understood she'd been knocked out, and the fall and her heart not being quite at the peak did the rest. You don't think she had her hooks into anyone?"

"Dark secrets in a minister's past," mused Bessie. "Oh, I don't think so. Mr. Ladd's only been married for about four years—Florrie's his second wife . . ."

"No hanky-panky about the first Mrs. Ladd's departure?" Crook suggested.

"I wouldn't know. What a trier you are, Mr. Crook. Mr. Ladd only came here about three years ago. And if there was anything, would she have left the money to the church?"

"Not one of these monomaniacs who thinks the end always justifies the means?"

"Knock Emily out for the sake of the money? We don't know that he even knew he'd get it. It was a bit of a surprise to everyone, I think, though Arthur did say she was going to tell the meeting something or other. We aren't that church ourselves," she explained.

"Arthur being Mr. Bastable? Yes, I've seen him. He put me on to you. Says she might have been meaning to get in touch with him, but if so she didn't make it."

"Poor Arthur. It was the local joke, or was before this happened, that Emily had set her cap for him. Mind you, I don't think it was true. I think she was too comfortable in her single state to want to change, and then she wasn't any chicken, and quite a bit older than he was. Anyway, Arthur's dodged too many designing females to be caught easily. And if he did marry again it would be someone like Paula Earl. It certainly won't be her fault if she doesn't become the second Mrs. Bastable."

"Mrs. Earl bein' . . . ?"

"The local Merry Widow. I must say Arthur could do a lot worse; and they did arrive at the party together. She said she just happened to be passing his house as he came out, so they walked down together, but . . ."

"I get you," said Crook. "An enterprising female has to give fate a bit of a shove sometimes. And, of course, a lady might stop to fasten a shoelace or something just as she got near the house."

"Mrs. Crook," began Bessie, but Crook shook his head. "No, ma'am, life's full of miracles, but that ain't one of them. No woman ever looked twice at me."

"And if she had she wouldn't have seen you for dust," contributed Bessie neatly. "Well, I wish I could help you. It would be a terrible thing if that boy is innocent and no one could prove it. But everything does seem to tie up, doesn't it?"

"A bit too neat for me," returned Crook. "I'm not one of your careful spinsters. It seems more natural to have a few loose ends. When things are too tidy I always suspect someone of giving nature a hand. Oh, and by the way," he added, "Bastable don't think Miss Foss was angling for a wedding ring? Too pleased with her own company, he thought?"

"You should ask Kate Winter what she thinks about that," Bessie advised him.

And "Many thanks, I will," said Crook.

Indefatigably he made his round of Burtonwood, followed by disbelieving stares at every step. In London he could melt into the landscape, or so he believed, but they'd never seen anyone like Arthur Crook in these parts before. His next port of call was the minister's house, where Mrs. Ladd answered his knock and regarded him with instant suspicion.

She was a round, trim little creature, a good deal younger than her husband, whose second wife she was. Their little daughter, aged three, stared at Crook and then began to chuckle.

"That's the ticket," said Crook. He put out a huge hand and the child grabbed it. "No critical sense at that age," he approved. "Your husband anywhere about?"

"He's busy at the moment." She regarded him warily.

"O.K.," said Crook. "I haven't come for a subscription." He explained his business. Mrs. Ladd looked startled. "Oh, but I thought the police had solved that. I can't believe anyone would deliberately murder old Miss Foss. She was very bossy, and she was rather a trial to Cyril, perpetually on the phone, and always insisting she must speak to him—sometimes you'd have thought she *was* the minister—but he soon learned to know her voice and passed her on to me as often as not. What an unmarried minister does I can't imagine. I tell Cyril sometimes he only married me to put a buffer between himself and the women of his congregation. As I say, she could be very irritating but you don't commit murder simply because someone annoys you."

"You'd be surprised," said Crook. "Still, I admit you do think twice. The police case is that X didn't give himself a chance for thinking twice. Whereas, if this was murder it was very prettily planned. And, as you say, you've got to be in a pretty hot spot to choose that way out. There is one other possibility," he admitted. "She might have got hold of some story the chap concerned didn't want circulated. Suppose there wasn't a letter or anything in the Reverend's post that morning."

Mrs. Ladd shook her head. "As a matter of fact, there was nothing except the figures about the church, and we could have done without them. All this burnishing of the outside of the cup, as he puts it, drives Cyril half mad. The first apostles weren't always worrying about pillars and tiled pulpits, he says. In fact, the whole world was their pulpit. Anyway, Miss Foss wasn't exactly handy with a pen. Believed in the personal touch—direct action was her word for it."

"And in the end it caught up with her." Crook looked grave. "Ever come across the nephew?" he asked.

"No. But he was in London that day, wasn't he?"

"People have to come back from London. Still, the police seem to have gone over him pretty well." He didn't want to start a rumor that might have no foundation at all. "Pity we don't know what the old lady meant to confide the following night."

The next name on his list was Miss Tremellen, but she had nothing to add to what she had told the police. At first she mistook Crook for a reporter and was prepared to be belligerent.

"What I've put up with from them," she said. "It's not my fault if my next-door neighbor gets herself murdered. It doesn't mean I want my picture in the paper, too."

"They've got to pull down their daily bread the

same as you or me," offered Crook, extenuatingly.

"But I couldn't *tell* them anything."

"You told them she set out alone. That was a lot of help. You see, the gate not being properly shut might have argued that someone had gone along with her who didn't know its tricks. You're dead sure she *was* alone?"

"Absolutely certain. To tell you the truth, I wanted to see what she looked like dressed up like a plush horse, as my nephew puts it, but it was rather dark and I couldn't see much. In fact, if I hadn't known who she was, I daresay I wouldn't even have realized it was Miss Foss, except perhaps by her walk. She moved as if someone had just wound her up; even in the shop she had a sort of stiffness. There was a light burning in the house," she added.

"You're sure it *was* Miss Foss you saw?"

"Oh, yes, I feel certain it was. Anyway I should have heard the door slam again—if she had come out later, I mean. Sound does carry so in these narrow streets—and she'd naturally leave the light on to give the impression the house wasn't empty."

Coming away from Love Street he ran into Dinah James.

"Have you found out anything yet?" she asked, excitedly.

"Solving a crime's like making a hasty pudding," Crook assured her. "You put in all the ingredients and stir 'em well together and hope you get the right result. Matter of fact, I haven't got all my ingredients yet. I'm still shopping for them."

Shopping seemed to be the appropriate word. It was in Laker, the dairy, that he ran into Kate Winter.

She was a pleasant middle-aged woman in whom a lively curiosity was decently veiled.

"Mr. Bastable told me someone was going around asking questions," she said frankly. "Mind you, it was a shocking thing, and if the police are right it could happen to any of us."

"Not if you don't take the week's housekeeping money around with you after dark," Crook assured her.

"How that young fellow knew she had all that money in her bag beats me," Kate confessed.

"My point is he didn't," said Crook, swooping like a bird of prey on this minute mouse. "He didn't know because he'd never set eyes on her and wouldn't have attacked her if he had."

"I don't know about that." Kate sounded guarded. "He doesn't seem a very steady sort of young fellow."

"There's a whale of a difference between not sticking to jobs and hitting an old girl over the head," Crook pointed out. "What the police don't seem to have taken into account is that this could have been a personal crime. I mean, say someone had it in for her and saw his or her chance . . ."

"Emily was always asking for trouble; I've told her so myself more than once, but she wasn't the kind that takes advice. A nagger, that's what I'd call her. Why can't you keep your conscience to yourself? I'd ask."

"Conscience?" Crook picked up his big ears.

"That's right. There was a case a few years back

when Mr. Prendergast was minister. There was a girl at the house then that had been in a bit of trouble some time back. Light-fingered, that was her difficulty. Miss Foss got to know about it, don't ask me how, and she thought it was her duty to warn Mrs. Prendergast. The minister had money, the chapel money as well as his own sometimes, lying about the house. 'You haven't any right to take risks with that,' she said. 'Mind you, I'm not saying the girl would make that mistake another time, but if she knows you've heard about her first fall she'll be more careful.' She told Mr. Bastable, too."

"Why, the girl didn't work for him, did she?"

"No. But she said she thought it was her duty. 'Can't you let other people be?' I asked her. 'Most of us have got something in our past we'd as lief not share with others.' 'Not me,' she said. 'I've always been as open as the day.'"

"I've met plenty of days I wouldn't mind giving a miss," agreed Mr. Crook. "What happened—about the girl, I mean?"

"Mrs. Prendergast was ready enough to keep her. 'It's all right, Annie,' she said. 'You've been six months with us and you've done well. You can be sure we shall never throw this up against you.' But, of course, the girl didn't stop. 'It doesn't give me a chance,' she said to me. 'If anything's ever missing they'll know it was me, though that Mrs. Hale they've got helping now isn't too careful about whose sugar she takes home with her.' 'As you sow, so you shall reap' was all Miss Foss said. No, I don't know what happened to Annie.

She didn't stay in these parts. But she was like that—Emily Foss, I mean—always nosing out things about other people and then doing her duty as she saw it."

"Every virtue but charity," agreed Mr. Crook. "Like living in a house where you can't ever draw the curtains."

"One day, I told her, you'll find out a bit too much and then you'll wish you'd been born with a shorter tongue. Mind you, she was right when she said she hadn't anything to hide. Honest as anyone could look for. I've known her to walk half a mile to return a penny she'd overcharged. And clean—the place was spotless. Only she couldn't help but interfere. Why, she even came to me once, told me she was speaking as a friend and it might be a good thing if I was to look around for another job."

"Give you any reason?" asked Crook.

"Oh, her meaning was clear enough. Had her eye on Mr. Bastable, everyone knew that. Called him up every excuse she could think of, didn't think anything of coming in with or without an invitation. What's wrong with the mail? I said to her once. But she said there were some things best not put on paper. Other people besides me noticed that," went on Kate, her brow darkening. "Made a proper monkey of herself over him. Well I know there's plenty here wouldn't mind becoming Mrs. B., but if you ask me he hasn't any wish to change his state. And if he had he'd be the first to give me warning. Know what he calls me—joking, of course? The lion in the way. 'Some people keep pet dogs,' he'll say, laughing, 'and some prefer cats, but give me a lion.' "

Crook thought that if all lions looked as amicable and competent as this one you could go a long way farther and choose a less amenable pet.

"And if he was to consider an offer," Kate continued, "it wouldn't have been Emily Foss. Why, she was ten years and more older than him."

Crook went off, thinking hard. He was learning a lot about the dead woman. She was nosy; she had the sort of conscience that, unable to find grounds for troubling its owner, makes trouble for others; she had a knack of discovering other people's weak spots. There might be half a dozen people in Burtonwood who breathed a good deal more comfortably when they heard she'd gone to a world where perhaps her good qualities would be more appreciated. You couldn't tell Crook anything about camouflage. He knew murder can hide behind a smiling face as much as Providence, he knew that sudden temptation can seize on and defeat the most normal of citizens. It was one of his theories that murderers aren't a class apart, as so many people seem to imagine, but chaps like you and me, bringing the wife back a box of chocolates on payday and taking the boy to sail his boat of a Sunday. Suppose Emily had probed to the heart of someone's mystery and wasn't prepared to keep her mouth shut? Opening her mouth seemed to be her particular weakness. Well then, that widened the field immeasurably. Because if there'd been as much as a hint it was bound to have come out by this time, not necessarily to the police, but around the village. He kept his ears open in the pub and on the green and just hanging about in the shops. It didn't surprise him now that Emily should have been knocked on the head, and he was more than ever inclined to believe it was someone she had known rather than a boy snatching a ratty old purse that didn't look as if it held more than a pound or so at most.

He thought he was pretty well through with his inquiries at Burtonwood; he hadn't left a stone unturned, even going to the office of the local bus company to pursue his inquiries there. He learned, as he had anticipated, that the only accident in which one of the company's vehicles had been involved had been on the day of Emily's disaster, which seemed to give him a pretty clear lead as to Mount's movements that afternoon.

"I'd have been back earlier but for the accident," he'd said to the police.

Well, he couldn't see any other step he could usefully take. He telephoned Bill in London, but there was nothing to be learned at that end, so he hopped into the Old Superb and made his way to Elsham.

NINE

It was a Wednesday, early closing day for the neighborhood, a fact that suited him down to the ground. He reached the jeweler's shop at about a quarter to one. It was well situated on a bus route and close to a stop. There were no dress emporia near at hand to distract the wandering eye, and it seemed to him that a lady waiting for the infrequent bus might well have her attention distracted by the well laid out trays of attractively priced goods in the window. Say she saw a pair of earrings or a brooch that caught her fancy she might step in, and, not wanting to miss her bus, which meant waiting half an hour for the next, clinch a bargain on the spot. "That situation worth five hundred pounds a year to him, I wouldn't wonder," Crook told himself as he pushed open the door and saw there was no one in the shop but a woman cashier, seated behind a sort of cage on one side. She had not so much said farewell to youth and beauty as by-passed them altogether. She didn't offer to move when Crook came in, closing the door firmly behind him; her experienced glance summed him up.

Watch strap, four-and-six. That was obviously how she classed him.

"Can I help you?" she asked in an unenthusiastic way.

"When rose leaves of December the frosts of June shall fret," reflected Mr. Crook, who had a store of similar quotations at his finger tips.

He strolled across and looked at a showcase that was also the counter. Attractively priced watches and small alarm clocks, and second-hand stuff that must have been salvaged when the Ark came to rest on Mount Ararat, he reflected. Brooches and tiepins and dangling earrings—he wondered who would ever buy them. Alongside was a tall glass cabinet full of highly polished silver cream jugs and teapots, basins, cruets; there was even a circular blue velvet pincushion girdled with filigree that held his especial attention.

He turned to find Miss Fry watching him.

"Is there something I can show you?" she repeated, and this time she did make a feint of moving.

"Boss anywhere around?" asked Crook.

She drew a sharp breath. "If you mean Mr. Mount, he's out."

"Maybe I could wait."

She looked meaningly at the grandfather clock Sidney wouldn't sell.

"This is early closing day. Mr. Mount isn't likely to be back before one."

"Maybe I should go up to his private address," Crook offered.

Her patience broke. "If you want to make an appointment with Mr. Mount you should write," she suggested.

"I'm only over for the day," Crook offered. "And my business is personal. I reckon I'll wait."

Without warning, she broke into violent speech.

"Are you another of them?" she demanded. "Oh, why can't you leave him alone? What good do you think you're going to do yourself by ruining him?"

"I never said anything about ruin," protested a startled Mr. Crook.

"If you make him sell the shop, how does that help you? Just killing the goose that lays the golden eggs. And that's what will happen if you don't give him a break. You might think he'd had enough trouble—Mrs. Mount being a refugee and never really getting over it and Paul being delicate—he wants more consideration than most men, not less."

Crook looked at her thoughtfully. He knew most women are ace actresses, and was generous enough to acknowledge that nine times out of ten it was as well for them that they were. He was remembering another quotation about the lady protesting too much. After all, it didn't seem natural that she should open up within the first five or ten minutes to a stranger, without even knowing what his business really was. He turned his back on the showcase and asked quite gently, "You got anything against Mr. Mount?"

Her amazement was so obviously genuine that he acquitted her at once. She really had meant what she said just now, was desperately concerned for her employer. Her next words explained her attitude. It was as an employer that she thought of him, not as a friend or a human being, and certainly not as a lover.

"What an idiotic thing to say. Of course I haven't. And if you want to know, it's myself I'm thinking about quite as much as him. Mind you, I hate to see him in this state. He's always treated me well, and he hasn't made excuses like a lot of men would to get in someone a bit younger. I've held this job for ten years, and I expected to stay in it till I draw my pension. It was one thing during the war when people couldn't get help because of the army, but things have changed now; once admit you're forty and you've bought it. Oh, they tell you it's the insurance people, they even tell you that if they haven't got a contributory pension scheme. What they mean is they want the girls, though why they should, seeing they don't do half the work and never have a thought in their minds beyond boys . . ."

Crook gently steered her back to her original course. "I don't want to make the boss's life a burden to him," he began, and she interrupted excitedly. "Then why do you go on harrying him? You're not the police?" she added sharply.

"You ask them," suggested Crook with a grin.

"Anyway we've had them. Not that Mr. Mount could tell them anything. He and his aunt didn't see much of each other. Why, she as good as told him he was a traitor marrying that German widow. We had a bomb once during the war—just the one—and she believed to the day of her death it was Mrs. Mount tipping them off."

"As I say," repeated Crook as she paused for breath, "I don't want to make trouble for him, but there's others to be considered."

"And I suppose you've only to look in the glass to see who they are," she retorted.

Crook looked at her with genuine admiration. He yielded to no one in his pleasure at the snappy comeback.

"Well, not exactly," he said. "My client . . ."

"Here is Mr. Mount," exclaimed Miss Fry in a conspiratorial tone. As the tall thin figure opened the shop door and entered, doffing a black hat as he crossed the threshold, Crook thought, "This chap's mistaken his vocation. He should have gone in for undertaking. There's a profession where you never lack customers."

Mount came forward, pulling off his gloves, hanging his hat on a peg and saying, "Did you want to see me?" He looked questioningly at Miss Fry. "This gentleman," he began . . .

"He's not a customer," said Miss Fry rather shrilly. "He wants to see you on private business."

There was never much color in Sidney Mount's face; now it looked like curdled cream.

"I hope I haven't kept you waiting," he said, but there was a tightness in his voice that betokened the strain under which he was laboring.

"I've all the time there is," Crook assured him. "After all, there's always tomorrow, and that's a brand-new day."

Mount glanced at the grandfather clock. "I don't think we need anticipate any more customers now, Miss Fry," he said. "We will close for the day."

Expecting trouble, decided the astute Mr. Crook. Now why?

Miss Fry's hands, collecting the invoices with which she had been dealing, shook so that she had difficulty in assembling them in a neat stack. Mount stood in the middle of the floor, watching her. Crook looked at the little alarm clocks in the glass case. But out of the corner of his eye he saw the troubled bookkeeper rescue from some dark corner what appeared to his fascinated gaze to be a pudding basin roughly covered in sand-colored felt, and ram it on her head. She picked up a bag that was approximately a twin to the one owned by Miss Foss, an umbrella and a library book and hurried out. Mr. Mount followed her to the door, shut and locked it, and turned the notice OPEN so that it now proclaimed CLOSED. This done he turned to Crook and said, "We'll go into my office. Then perhaps you'll tell me who you are."

"Crook's the name, Arthur Crook. Take my card. A lawyer," he added, tugging one out of his pocket.

"A lawyer?" The sparse black brows lifted. "Representing whom?"

"Chap called Leonard Hunter. I see you know the name."

"That's the fellow they've taken for the murder of Miss Foss."

"I'm glad you put it that way. I get tired correcting chaps who say, 'That's the chap who put out the old lady's light.'"

"Is there any difference?" demanded Mount, pulling out a straight-backed chair standing in front of a desk, and taking a second one himself.

"Only the difference between wet and dry, heaven

and hell, life and death. You see, I'm here to see what assistance I can get from you to show that the young chap don't *have* to be guilty."

There was no questioning the amazement in Mount's voice when he heard that.

"I hadn't realized there was any question of reopening the case. Why, there's been a trial and a verdict . . ."

"So he's got something on his plate besides the murder of his aunt," thought Crook, shrewdly.

"So you'll see there ain't much time to lose," he pointed out smoothly, "and when in doubt come to the fountainhead."

"The fountainhead?" Mount sounded more perplexed than ever.

"Well, you knew the old lady, which is more than my client did. And, as I said just now, we've got to get a hustle on because the time's getting short. Oh, fourteen days may seem a whale of a time when you're waiting to go on your summer holiday, but to a boy who knows the last of them is going to write finis to his history, they go by like a dream, a bad dream," he wound up, emphatically.

"I'm still at a loss," confessed Mount, and indeed he did look utterly bewildered. "How you think I can help you, I mean. I never set eyes on this fellow, Hunter, until after my aunt's death . . ."

"And it's my job to show that he didn't set eyes on her even then," capped Crook, neatly. "Now, if it wasn't him, it was someone else. I can believe a lot of things but not that Miss Foss committed suicide, so it seems likely she had a secret enemy; and equally likely you'd know more about her than the neighbors."

"There, I assure you, you're mistaken," Mount told him. "However much or little such persons can assist you"—Crook wished the fellow wouldn't talk like a tract—"the odds are that any one of them can be of more help at this juncture than myself. As I reluctantly was compelled to inform the police, the relations between my aunt and myself were of an exceedingly formal nature. She had what seemed to me the gross impertinence to disapprove of my wife on the grounds of nationality alone—she gave herself no opportunity of getting acquainted—and things actually reached a pitch where either refused to meet the other. Meetings between us of recent years were exceedingly few and far between."

"Quite understandable," murmured Crook, sympathetically.

"Miss Foss came here on August Bank Holiday to bring the brooch she intended for the young lady's twenty-first birthday present, and I visited her when I returned it. On neither occasion was my wife present. Since that day we have had no communication."

"Not even the day she died?" murmured Crook.

Sidney Mount's head jerked around toward him. "What do you mean by that?"

"I mostly mean what I say," Crook retorted mildly. "Look, there's no sense our playing 'Here we go round the Mulberry-bush,' and no time either. Let me put you in the picture, and when I've put some cards on the table, maybe you'll follow suit. I know for one thing that you were in Burtonwood that Friday, and you could have been with her at the approximate time of her death."

"Who says that?"

"I ain't Euclid," acknowledged Crook, "but even at my sort of school they taught us how to add two and two. You were on the bus from Finney's Bridge that came into collision with a motorcyclist. Well, you told the police yourself there'd been an accident which brought you back here later than you expected, and that's the only one on record."

Grudgingly Mount acceded the point. "The train service is most unsatisfactory from Finney's Bridge. I usually take the bus on my rare excursions to London."

"And you traveled right through to Elsham on that bus? Is that your story?"

"Why should you doubt it?"

"Because it reached Elsham at seven o'clock, but you didn't pick up your wife till seven-thirty. You're not going to tell me you opened up the shop for that extra half-hour. No, you changed at Burtonwood to the small local bus, and it got you here at seven-twenty-five and you went straight from the station to collect Mrs. Mount."

"You seem very sure of my movements," said Mount, scornfully.

"All part of the Arthur Crook service. I've been up to the bus company office at Burtonwood and there were only three passengers made the complete journey right through from Finney's Bridge and you weren't one of them."

"I—I preferred not to remain on the original bus. There was broken glass on the floor and a considerable draft. I thought I should be more comfortable on another vehicle."

"That's as may be," said Crook obstinately. "Only, you didn't know there was going to be an accident, did you? So why only book to Burtonwood? Because that's what you did. I've seen the Bus Company's records," he added quickly.

This was bluffing with a vengeance and if Mount called it Crook was back where he started. But Mount had the guilt consciousness of all men with something to hide, so he only said weakly, "Well, it's true. I did get off at Burtonwood, but you can't make anything of that. I didn't see my aunt."

"No?" said Crook, unemphatically. "How come?"

"She was out at a party, as you very well know."

"Ah, but *you* didn't know that when you arrived. You've said as much to the police."

"Dear me, Mr. Crook, your memory seems remarkably short," rebuked his companion. "I explained a few minutes ago that my aunt and I were on the coolest of terms. She would scarcely have informed me of her plans in any case, in addition to which she was so urgent about the repairs to the brooch when she brought it on the August Bank Holiday that I certainly gained the impression that the party in question was a matter of days. If I'd known that the party wasn't to be given until November, I wouldn't have put myself out the way I did. It didn't surprise me that my aunt never wrote to say the girl was pleased with the thing, admired the new setting. She never used a postage stamp if she could help it."

"So, knowing it was Friday and Friday was her day for doing the accounts—oh yes, even you must have known that much—you thought you'd beetle along and have a word with her. Care to tell me why?"

"No." The word shot out like a machine-gun bullet. "I absolutely refuse to discuss my personal affairs with you. They are my concern—and Mrs. Mount's, of course."

Crook remembered Miss Fry's outburst. "In a bit of a jam, aren't you?" he asked quite casually. "No, it's no use blaming the lady secretary. She has your interests at heart, but seeing she ain't blind or dumb, she'd be bound to realize everything wasn't running as smooth as an ebb tide."

"If you have been cross-examining Miss Fry . . ."

"Examining," murmured Crook. "No, not that either. She simply wanted me to go away and leave you in peace, pointed out there wasn't much sense killing the goose that laid the golden eggs. I don't know anything about golden eggs and I couldn't care less, but I don't mean to have Lennie Hunter hamstrung to make a hangman's holiday."

Mount seemed to catch fire from his belligerent mood. "And I don't intend to have my wife's affairs made the common talk of the town. You've never been a refugee, never been hounded out of your home, and seen everyone—every single person—who makes up your private life butchered under your eyes."

Even Crook sobered a bit at that. "I'm sorry," he

said, "truly I am, but the fellow you should have it in for is Hitler, not me, and he's gone to his account. . . . So she was one of his victims," he added reflectively.

"She lost her mother and both her young brothers through treachery," Mount said in a deep and desperate voice. "They were hidden with some other persons of Jewish origin and told to await their rescuers on a particular day and to answer a particular signal. The day came, the signal was given . . ." He stopped, as though he couldn't complete the sentence.

"And—someone sold them up the river?" completed Crook. "That's an awful thing, I admit. Your Miss Fry said something about Mrs. Mount being a widow . . ."

"Her husband's body was found in his lodging a few days later. He'd been shot. After that she had no one —still has no one—but myself. I was involved with a —well, I suppose you could call it a resistance movement in Germany in 1938—quite a lot of us were out there trying to smuggle the victims out—that's how I met Else—subsequently she married me. I'll put this on record, Mr. Crook. I married her for love, no question of pity or wanting her to have a British passport, nothing like that. I wanted to make up as well as I could for all she'd suffered. I brought her here and after a time we had Paul—my son . . ."—his voice softened, the cold eyes glowed—"and I began to think she was forgetting. It takes a long time to forget what she saw. If she hadn't gone back to get some papers she'd have shared the fate of the others; as it was she saw it from the window and escaped from the back. She wanted to get hold of her husband, warn him what had happened . . ." He stopped, drawing his hand across his corpselike brow.

"You've pretty well spiked my guns," Crook acknowledged. "I wish you'd try and believe I haven't got a thing against you personally or your wife, only —my job is to show that someone else could have been responsible for Miss Foss's death. It would be best, of course, if I could show who that someone actually was, but if I can stir up an element of doubt that'll do the trick. And I know, what at present the police don't, that you were in Burtonwood that night, with the intention of seeing your aunt."

Mount stared at him. "And do you mean, after what I've told you, and it's a thing I've not repeated to three people in nearly twenty years, you're still going ahead? Haven't you any human feelings at all? Can't you realize how the press are going to descend on this like—like vultures?" He looked thunderstruck. "I'm a married man and a father. I've got my living to consider. You know so much you probably know that this business of mine is all I have to support the three of us. If there's even a hint, a shred of suspicion attached to my name, I'm finished. Murder's an ugly charge." He shivered.

"So my client's found out. As for being a husband and father, well, it's up to me to see young Hunter gets the chance of following in your footsteps, the same as any other innocent man."

"So my reputation means nothing to you?" Mount seemed flabbergasted.

"You ain't paying me to protect it," Crook pointed out, inexorably.

"And this young—ruffian—is?" His pinched nostrils sharpened, like some wild creature scenting blood. "That's an odd thing, isn't it? As I remember it, Hunter had no means at all. His lawyer and counsel were provided out of public funds."

"These things can be arranged," Crook murmured. "I wouldn't say I was fussy, but I'm a member of the community that pays taxes, and I don't begrudge him what he had, particularly as it didn't seem to do him much good."

"If you're looking for proof that I was involved you're wasting your time," said Mount, tight-lipped. "It doesn't exist, and you know it."

"Do I? All I know at present is that you got out at Burtonwood and went to see your aunt."

"Who wasn't at home."

"But you went to the house?"

"Yes. But there was no answer when I rang the bell. Though there was a light burning in the hall. I could see that through the glass."

"And when she didn't come, it didn't occur to you to rouse one of the neighbors and find out if she'd conked out or anything?"

"I had no reason to suppose anything of the kind. I knew she had a horror of burglars and I supposed that was why she wouldn't open the door at such an hour. It was quite dark and raining."

"So you just went away again?"

"Obviously."

"Without seeing a soul?"

"It was hardly the kind of night you'd expect people to be abroad."

"So what it boils down to is—no one actually saw you go up to the door?"

Mount looked puzzled. "Presumably not. At all events, no one's come forward to say so."

"And afterwards? You didn't pay any other visits?"

"I have no acquaintances in Burtonwood."

"Didn't drop into the Fox and Hounds or the Seven Moons for a drop of you-know-what and happen to mention you'd been calling on Miss Foss?"

Mr. Mount flinched. "I am not a drinking man. I should have welcomed a cup of tea, but I could find no place open. I merely walked up to the bus station and waited for my bus."

"Didn't manage to get a cuppa tea there, I take it?"

"The refreshment room was closed."

"Or speak to anyone?"

"Certainly not."

"So what it amounts to is you can't produce a soul to back up one single statement you've made."

"Why on earth should I wish to?"

"Never read your Dickens? 'Sammy, Sammy, vy worn't there an alleybi?'"

"I don't require an alibi. You haven't an iota of proof."

"It's a funny thing," offered Crook, "but when it comes down to brass tacks, the police haven't got any proof either—against Lennie Hunter, I mean. They got their verdict on the strength of a weak story, a silly attitude on his part, and some very useful coincidences."

"Nevertheless, a jury considered it conclusive."

"Oh, juries'll think anything," was Crook's casual reply.

"And I repeat, for the last time, that I did not see my aunt that night."

"Hunter says the same, and look where it's got him. And the police are bound to think it a bit odd you didn't mention calling that night, or bein' in Burtonwood at all, come to that. Now, tell me something else. The lady hadn't said she'd be phoning you that evening?"

"Phoning me? Why on earth should she? Anyway, I was in London and my wife was out. And perhaps you've forgotten, my aunt had no telephone."

"But it's common knowledge she always used the one in the Court. Still not going to tell me why you wanted to see her? Right, I'll tell the story and you correct me as and when you want to. You needed money—yes, of course you did—and she was your only hope. You expected to get what she left . . ."

"And I still shall," insisted Mount, excitedly. "My lawyer has the matter in hand. She had no rights over that money, it was earned by my grandfather . . ."

"We-ell, wouldn't you say Miss Foss did a good deal of the earning herself? Nurse and handmaiden to the old gentleman for years, and worked like a beaver ever since his death, by all accounts. The law allows her to leave her money any way she pleases . . ."

"Her father would turn in his grave . . ."

"That's his privilege. Now, let's get back to our muttons. You were being pushed for cash, there was the prospect you might have to sell the shop which, as you've just pointed out, is all that stands between you and government welfare—so obviously you'd look around for a backer. And the choice wasn't a very wide one. You say you never got inside the house —well, I'm prepared to believe that."

"Then what is all this about?" demanded the harassed jeweler.

"The police have an idea that maybe her attacker was waiting for her in the Court, possibly even inside the telephone booth. There's no record that she let out a yell . . ."

"She could hardly hope to be heard in any case. That booth is in a very isolated position . . ."

"I see you remember the setup, though you haven't been in the neighborhood for quite a while."

"As a matter of fact, I used that telephone booth myself to put through a call to my wife when I was in Burtonwood—in August," he added hurriedly.

"You think of everything, don't you? Well, to continue with my story. If Miss Foss had been confronted with a stranger who looked threatening, you'd expect her to scream or something. But if it was someone she recognized, why then she'd be the perfect lady. Fancy seeing you. What are you doing here?"

"I can see you intend to involve me at all costs," said Mount, grimly. "I can assure you it won't benefit that young ruffian who, if he were permitted to live, would simply go from one act of violence to another and spend the rest of his days as a public charge."

"I ain't concerned with morals, only with murder," Crook said in a rather exhausted voice. The next moment a step was heard on the staircase beyond, and the inner door opened.

The woman who entered must have been a looker in her time, thought Crook. She still bore the remnants of a haggard and distinctive beauty. When she saw Crook she stopped short. He pulled himself to his feet. Mount seemed numbed by her arrival.

"Mrs. Mount? I'm afraid I've kept your husband. A matter of business."

"It is nearly twenty minutes past one," said Mrs. Mount, paying no attention to the stranger. "You know you cannot afford to play tricks with your digestion, Sidney. This is early closing day. I should have expected anyone to know that."

"Let me introduce myself," said Crook without a shred of hesitation. "Crook's the name, and I'm here in Lennie Hunter's interest."

"Lennie Hunter?"

"My dear Else, you must remember. He is the young man . . ."

"Of course I remember who he is. But why has Mr. Crook come to you? You had never heard his name until everyone heard it."

"That's what I thought," Crook agreed. "I just

wondered if your husband could give me any hints about the lady. Someone might have had it in for her . . ."

"Have you reason to suppose anything of the sort?" demanded Mrs. Mount.

"Well, I'm workin' on the theory that she was killed because somebody meant her to die, not because a bag snatcher saw his chance and hit harder than he intended. And, unless you're a lunatic, you don't go around committing murder for fun. Say she had a secret in her life . . ."

"Miss Foss?"

"You'd be surprised. Well, these quiet livers have to burst out sometime. Ever noticed that practically all the people writing poison-pen letters are outwardly respectable, middle-aged women who've been battening down their disappointments under hatches for years and suddenly the lid blows off? Think of the poor lady's existence. Looking after Poppa—and that doesn't sound exactly a joy ride—and after that working in the shop and spending her free time at church."

"If there *was* anything, we could not tell you," Else Mount assured him fiercely. "She was almost a stranger. I thought the police had decided she was killed for her money."

"That's the second time I'm agreeing with them in five minutes," said Crook. "Question is, who needed her money most?"

"Whoever needed it was unlikely to get it except by force. She would not have parted with five pounds to save a life. My husband can tell you that. Only a fortnight before her death—you remember her words?" Her deep voice became deeper yet. Like having a lady bloodhound on the premises, thought Mr. Crook. 'There have been too many wolves in sheep's clothing—I would not give five shillings to any refugee society on earth, not if it was to bring them into this country'—and of course when she said that she was thinking of me and my son. Oh, she was a wicked woman, she deserved to be murdered. If I could save that young man I would. Why should he have to die on her account?"

"He ain't going to, not if I can prevent it," said Crook. "Now, lady, this time you spoke of, two weeks before she died—that was when she said the bit about the wolf in sheep's clothing—said it to you, did she?"

"I never met her for nearly two years," cried the woman, proudly. "When she came here I was out, or at least I stayed in my room. I can tell you, it does a businessman no good to have a relative calling who looks as if she had been dressed out of a ragbag. She was a disgrace to the shop. Fortunately it must have been clear to anyone who saw her that she was mad."

"If she made that remark to your husband I'd not be surprised if he was mad, too," said Crook sympathetically. "Only two weeks before she died, eh?"

"My dear Else, you are confused," cried Sidney desperately. "And you will confuse Mr. Crook. It's true," he added, "that she did say something of the kind, but it was on an earlier occasion."

"It was on that occasion that you told me," the

woman insisted, "when you went to see her. Why do you look at me like that, Sidney? What does it matter if Mr. Crook knows you called on her that day? That was not the day she died."

Mount rose and with a tenderness that transformed his gaunt pale face guided her out of the room.

"I will be up soon," he promised, "very soon." He closed the door and the two men stood in silence, listening to the feet going up the stairs. They moved like the feet of destiny, thought Crook, who was not commonly given to such flowery notions. Why on earth did she have to butt in then? Though it was a good bit of luck for us that she did.

"Now, don't say it," he counseled Mount, as a distant door closed. "Your lady has let the cat out of the bag, and if you don't want it mewing on the steps of the police station you'll start talking sense. You went to see Miss Foss two weeks before she died, because you wanted some help. And she didn't give it you. And two weeks later you went to see her again . . ."

"And she wasn't in."

"That's your last word?"

"To you or to the police or to the Recording Angel," said Mount violently.

"And you didn't write when you found she wasn't at home? And yet you were desperate enough . . ."

"You are ignoring the time factor. Even if I had wished to write there was no opportunity. The mail had gone for that day, and the next morning the police came to tell me she was dead. Anyway, there are some things it is best not to commit to paper. No, all your trouble is wasted. She was killed by the young man who has been condemned to death. Why you should interest yourself in the matter is your affair. I can only repeat what I have already told you. If he did not kill her, who did?"

"Is that a challenge?" asked Crook, standing up and looking around for his bright brown bowler. "I'll meet you. Give me a few more days and I'll be able to tell everyone who put out her light. And it won't be only the police whose faces will be red."

He turned to go, but Mount was before him. "I will say one last word, Mr. Crook, and it is worth listening to. You will be well advised to leave the matter alone. I warn you, if you don't, you may regret it, regret it very strongly indeed."

"Are you threatening to murder me?" asked Crook. "You must be in pretty deep."

The change in Sidney Mount was horrifying. He had looked driven enough before, now his face was suddenly dark.

"Sometimes," he said, "a murder may be justified."

"Take the word of the man who knows," said Crook. "That game ain't ever worth the candle. If you had someone else in mind, one of your other visitors . . ."

"My other visitors?" Mount's hand dropped limply to his side.

"If you don't want things to leak out you should employ a deaf-mute to keep your accounts," Crook warned him. "And don't go around and stick a dagger into Miss Fry. She's on your side."

"My visitors, as you call them, are simply men of business who represent the landlord," Mount said and his voice was as ghostly as his face. Crook had never seen anyone who changed color so easily. "You are, as they say, barking up the wrong tree if by some feat of imagination you connect them with my aunt's death. And now I must rejoin my wife. You can see for yourself, she is getting anxious."

He led the way into the shop, unlocked the door and opened it cautiously. The street was empty, and when he saw that he breathed more freely.

"Remember what I have told you, Mr. Crook. A desperate man is capable of desperate deeds."

TEN

Crook crossed the street to the Old Superb, got in and sat so still at the wheel that some urchins who had come to mock sheered off, feeling uncomfortable. Crook noticed neither their presence nor their withdrawal. His whole mind was obsessed by a conviction that he was about to learn something of stupendous importance and the fact that Mount would place every conceivable obstacle in the way of his learning it.

"That chap's at his last gasp," he was thinking. "Of course, he couldn't guess his Frau was going to let down the side like that. He knows a whole lot more than he's ready to admit."

He recalled Mount's story about his wife, very moving, very tragic, but, face it, quite unproved. It could all be true, but it could equally be a fandango of romantic fiction. All that seemed certain was that the pair had met in Germany and at that time Mrs. Mount had been married to a fellow countryman.

Maybe Mount murdered the fellow himself, maybe he ain't dead at all but has suddenly decided to do an Enoch Arden and is putting on the screw. From the way they spoke of the boy I should say they're both devoted to him, and it's no fun to learn when you're just about going to your big school that you're a little basket—a mongrel basket at that.

Suppose that last conjecture were right, and the real husband was threatening to pull down the roof unless he was paid to keep his mouth shut? That would be an explanation of the mysterious visitors and Mount's look of anguish—no other word would do justice to his bearing. Naturally he wouldn't unbosom himself to Auntie, she'd make the obvious comeback—"You're not married to this woman, let her return to her husband." From all he had learned of Miss Foss he couldn't believe that sentiment would play any part in her outlook toward life or the woes of others. He remembered her saying about the unfortunate servant girl, that as a man sows so shall he reap. She would be perfectly capable of saying it to her nephew. Well, then, suppose Sidney had sprung her a cock-and-bull story about the shop being in difficulties, asked for a loan to tide him over. What was it Bastable had said? She was concerned about a threatened increase in her own rent, and everyone agreed that she was fond of money. On all counts, her nephew must have been absolutely desperate to have approached her in the first place. Presumably the unacknowledged visit two weeks before the old woman's death had been an attempt to raise the wind, and equally obviously she had refused. The police would have unearthed any sudden and unexplained payment. Well, then, was it likely he'd make a second attempt within the fortnight? Far more probable that, driven by desperation, he would conceal himself in the court and, staging an anonymous attack, put out the old woman's light in the firm belief that everything she had would accrue to her sole surviving relative. Of course, he wouldn't be able to realize his fortune right away, but in such circumstances lawyers were usually disposed to be generous, would agree to an advance on the estate. The more he considered it, the worse it looked for Sidney Mount. All the same, he, Crook, could make no move till he had more definite information. He remembered Mount's deathly pallor and the voice in which he had said, "Some murders are justifiable." He was clearly upset about his wife, so that the fate of a young man he would regard as worthless wouldn't weigh with him in the least. Crook threw in the clutch and the Superb glided away from the curb.

Clearly Mount had known nothing about the will, in fact he had admitted as much. The next step was to find out more about the mysterious visitor or visitors to whom Miss Fry had referred. Crook no longer had any doubt that Mount's actions—whatever form they took—stemmed from his relationship with Mrs. M. His next step was to put Harries on to watch the shop.

"Let me know who calls and find out if possible who the fellow is. I don't mean ordinary customers, of course, though there's nothing to stop this chap posing as one. Probably speak with a foreign accent, may come out of hours."

He was aware that he had to move as delicately as Agag and equally that there was not much time left if young Hunter was to be saved.

Next he called up Bill to find out anything he could about Mount's marriage. "He may have married her abroad, of course," he acknowledged. "On the other hand if she was smuggled over—he may have jumped through the hoop right away to put her in the clear. It was the better part of twenty years ago, so it won't be easy to dig anything out. But you might try Somerset House. Check up on the boy's birth, too, though I can't at the moment see how that's going to help." A fresh thought struck him. "I suppose bigamy couldn't be his trouble," he exclaimed. "I've been thinking mostly of her; she was a widow, lost her husband to the Nazis. Say he was in love—he'd met her out there —and knew her one chance was to have his name and nationality. He'd be—what age?—past thirty. Not a bit unlikely that there was a Mrs. Mount roaming around somewhere."

"Wouldn't she have surfaced by this time?" suggested Bill.

"You'd think so, I admit. But it could be she had a gentleman friend of her own. Anyway, no harm checking for a marriage prior to 1938. Harries is watching the house, and if there are any more mysterious callers he'll nail 'em. One way and another we've got to get this thing settled before any of us are much older. Once a chap's on his guard you can never foresee what's going to happen."

He was sitting in the Seven Moons that night when the door opened and Dinah James came in. She didn't make a sudden dart at him, just went to the counter and ordered herself half a pint (none of these sticky short drinks for her, Crook noted with approval) and quite casually brought it over to his table.

"What's that stuff you're drinking?" asked Crook rather suspiciously as she sat down.

"Shandy. If you have it made with ginger beer you hardly taste the beer. I don't really like drinks, but Lennie said it made him look soft going around with a girl who always asked for ginger, so I took this. I couldn't suggest gin and lime or anything (Crook shuddered) because they're so expensive. Mr. Crook, are you sure it's going to be all right?"

"Where's your faith?" asked Crook.

"There's so little time left. Have you got *anything?*"

"You don't solve murder in two shakes of a nanny goat's tail," Crook told her. "It's one foot in front of the other, one foot in front of the other and so to the top of the mountain."

"Then—you do know?"

"Sometimes the only way to get there is the process of elimination. Who couldn't have done it?"

"Oh, hundreds of people, I suppose. But there are still hundreds who could."

"Murder's quite a risk," Crook reminded her.

"People didn't like her. At least, that's what Kate says."

"Kate?"

"Kate Winter. I've got a job there just temporarily. Mrs. Raymond, who helps with the rough work, has sprained her wrist and Kate put an advertisement in a shop window and I answered it. I didn't know it was her, of course, but I thought if it was a private house there wouldn't be other girls there to be at me all the

time, about Lennie. It isn't that they mean to be un-
kind, but it's rather a thrill for them."

"And Kate took you on?"

"You needn't sound so surprised. Though come to
that I think it was mostly on your account. She said,
'Haven't I seen you somewhere before?' and I said I'd
been working at the Grill, so she sniffed and said,
'Sooner you than me, I like to know what I'm eating.
But it couldn't have been there because I never go inside the place.' And then she said, 'I know. You're the
girl who used to go around with that young Hunter
chap. Well, I hope this has been a lesson to you not to
let yourself get picked up.' Mr. Crook, I knew then
how easy it must be to commit murder. I felt I could
have pushed her through the window. But I didn't say
anything, because I thought Emily Foss having been a
visitor to the house, she might know something she
didn't know she knew and let it out. Doesn't it ever
happen that way?" she added, wistfully.

"Well, how do you think murderers are ever found
out? Of course it does."

"I said, 'Some people don't think he did it. Mr.
Crook doesn't.' "

"I should have sewn your mouth up before I left,"
groaned Crook. "What was her comeback to that?"

"She said, 'I can't think why he takes all the
trouble. Not that it surprises me specially. I daresay
there were plenty of people who were glad enough to
hear Emily Foss was out of the way. She was a
troublemaker, but that's no excuse.' Mr. Crook, did

she really think she was going to marry Mr. Bastable?"

"Why ask me?" said Crook, reasonably. "I never knew the lady. Is that what Kate says?"

"She says she behaved as if she were the mistress of the house already, giving orders and telling Kate it was time she thought about looking for another job. She sounds awfully bossy," added the girl, simply. "You'd have expected someone of her age to know that's no way to get a man. You want to have your own way, of course, but you have to let them think it's what they wanted all along."

"You're too young to be cynical," Crook grumbled. "I'll tell you who didn't mean Miss Foss to change her estate at his expense and that's Bastable."

"She was after him, though. Everyone knows that. You don't suppose he—oh no, he had an alibi. Well, then . . ."

"Now you've picked up your skirts and you're chasing after Kate," Crook complained. "You can't ever make women realize you've got to have some proof, that feminine intuition won't do the trick. Not that Kate couldn't have settled herself very comfortably elsewhere if Mr. Bastable had brought home a new Mrs. B."

"Ah, but perhaps he'd promised to leave her something handsome if she was in his service at the time of his death."

"You've been going to too many films. If that was what she had in mind, why didn't she drop a little arsenic in his coffee? From the look of them, I'd say his was the better life."

"Yes." She heaved a tremendous sigh. "I suppose so."

"You can't go chucking accusations at all and sundry," Crook warned her.

"I'd accuse the Archbishop of Canterbury if I thought it would do any good. Mr. Crook, are we really any farther on?"

"I've got my lines out," said Crook. He was troubled at the change in her; she was pale as a ghost, and there were dark smudges under her eyes. "You want some sleep," he told her abruptly.

"There'll be plenty of time to sleep later on. Mr. Crook, I went to see Lennie today."

"Indeed! And how many beans did you spill there?"

"I didn't get a chance. He wouldn't see me. I suppose he holds me responsible for all this. If I hadn't been late that day . . ."

"If he's that kind of a maniac I can't think why I'm spending all this time and effort trying to save him," said Crook in a cross voice. "He might be grateful to you for sticking by him. There's times I wonder why you do."

"Oh no, you don't mean that. You don't care for people because they're sensible or grateful or even fair. Mr. Crook, couldn't you go?"

"To the prison?" Crook looked staggered. "What for?"

"Just to let him know someone's rooting for him still."

"Probably wouldn't see me either."

"You could work it. I know you could."

"And what am I expected to say?"

"That it's going to be all right. You told me it would."

"And you think he's going to take that from a chap he never set eyes on before?"

"It would give him something to hold on to." She shivered uncontrollably, and the shandy glass shook in her hand, spilling the contents on the table.

"Here, you ain't going to turn on the waterworks, not here," protested Crook, genuinely alarmed.

"Of course not." Her voice shook as much as her hand. "It's just that I can't bear to think of him cooped up, never alone—he always hated being shut in, and those walls—he can't even see out of the window, can he? Why, unless things take a new turn he may never even see the sky again. I think of that at night when I can't sleep . . ."

"Oh, all right," said Crook grumpily. "If it'll ease your mind at all, I'll go and see the boy. But I warn you, it won't do any good. I told you, I've got my lines out and one day soon I'll reel 'em in and there'll be a fine fat fish gasping on the end."

"I don't care if you catch a whale unless you catch it before it's too late for Lennie," cried Dinah.

Crook caught George's sympathetic eye. "Two whiskeys and sodas," he said. "Just for once, sugar, you do what I say, and when you've downed it you go off home and get to bed. And if you know a druggist or doctor who'll give you anything to make you sleep, you pay him a little visit on the way."

There was nothing from Bill or Harries next morning so he supposed he might as well call around and meet his newest client.

Lennie Hunter stared at him sullenly. "You're not a new chaplain, are you?" he said, as Crook was ushered into his cell.

"Do I look like a chaplain?" asked Crook, without heat.

"Then you've come to the wrong number. I'm not expecting anyone."

"Not even the Angel of Hope? Now take it easy, and let me explain."

Lennie didn't let him get far. "This is all rot," he said. "Who asked you to butt in?"

"Now, look, even the police, who're your sworn enemies, don't want to hang an innocent man."

"You can't have met the police," suggested Lennie, dangerously polite.

"My job is to check up on one or two bits of fresh information we've managed to uncover. Mind you, I don't say they'll lead us anywhere, but they're all we've got."

"Can't think why you bother," said Lennie.

"Say I have an interest. You might even say I don't believe you did it."

For the first time Lennie looked straight at him through the separating grill. "You must be the only living person who doesn't."

"Don't be modest. There's Dinah James."

If you touch a hedgehog or a wood louse with your toe, it will curl up in a ball, the one exhibiting a fine

ANTHONY GILBERT

show of prickles, the other a suit of chain mail. Lennie
did the same.

"Dinah James?"

"If you were thinking of saying you've never met
her, think again. You can do with a pal or two at this
juncture."

"Was it she who dragged you into this?"

"Who else?"

Lennie swore. "You're shocking your guard,"
Crook murmured. "What's the matter? Are you so set
on the high jump . . . ?"

"I don't want Dinah dragged into this. It can't do
any good. She was in the court during the trial. I
thought once she was going to get up and speak . . ."

"Oh, she would, if it would have helped you, but she
didn't see that it could, and for once I agree with a
jane. You'd sworn there wasn't a girl, and if the prosecution could have shown there was it would simply
have strengthened their case. One lie proven shakes a
jury like the ague. In spite of everything she still be-
lieves in you, and what's more—and this is by way of
being a miracle—she's made me feel the same as her."

There was a moment's silence. Then Lennie said in a
voice so different that Crook almost jumped, "I didn't
do it, Mr. Crook. I was a fool to take the money, I
suppose . . ."

"Not the money," said Crook. "The pencil. And
even that may help in the end. A chap who's just committed a murder is hardly going to load himself with
the one thing that'll point the cops in his direction as

surely as the path of the righteous leads to the eternal day."

"I want my head examined," Lennie confessed frankly. "Once I heard she was a goner I should have chucked it away at once."

"So you most likely would have if you'd killed her, but you've got enough sense to see that's not the kind of thing you can urge in a court."

Lennie's face clouded over again. "Beats me how you think you're going to get those chaps to change their mind at this stage."

"I'm Arthur Crook," said Crook, simply. "Your young lady knows about me if you don't. Crook always gets his man. So keep your spirits up. By the way, I suppose you couldn't bring yourself to have another visitor?"

Immediately Lennie's face was as hard as granite. "Not if you mean Dinah. Best thing for her to do is forget about me, but if she has to remember it needn't be like this." He looked contemptuously at his surroundings. "I never meant her to come to the trial— the silly cow."

"When you're half as old as me," said Crook with a singular lack of delicacy, considering all the circumstances, "you'll know it's just a waste of breath tryin' to persuade women not to do what they've set their hearts on. And in this case I don't blame her. I wouldn't think much of her if she'd stayed away. Besides, she might have helped."

Lennie scowled; it was like the sudden fall of night.

"Well, I didn't want her to, see? A kid like that. She doesn't want her face all over the papers, and 'In Love With a Murderer' staring at her every time she passes a stand. Think I don't know? What's private feelings to these chaps? She's only a kid," he repeated. "She'll get over it."

"Lucky for you she's got more guts than you have," said Crook, brutally. "You've forgotten what women are like. Besides, if you've taken her fancy, why shouldn't she root for you?"

"She's a good kid," Lennie told him fiercely. "Kicked out of the house when she was sixteen because of that swine of a stepfather, could have gone to the bad right away for all they cared, hanging about coffee bars. Can't blame them if they do get picked up. Got to hear a human voice some time, haven't they? Now look here, mister, you go back and tell her if she wants to do something for me, she'll keep right out of this."

"Innocent, ain't you?" murmured Crook. "Every way, I mean. Be your age, son. Did you ever know a jane to keep out of trouble if she got the chance? Your young lady's in it up to the neck, and neck's the operative word. She's out to save yours, so keep your chin up and play a nice game of checkers with the guards if they want it. It ain't all jam for them, you know. You try and think what you'd feel like, night and day, night and day, watching a chap in your shoes. And they do it right around the clock. No sense making their job harder."

"You're bats," said Lennie. "Why on earth should I think of them?"

"It stops you thinking about yourself, and that can't be much fun. Well, be seeing you. Here comes the man with the watch. Time marches on."

Struck by the appositeness of this comment he made a rather hurried exit.

"You're going to have a surprise one day soon," he told the guard. "As sure as my name's Arthur Crook."

The guard moved back and spoke to Lennie. "Know who that was? Arthur Crook. Known as the criminal's hope. The human atom bomb's more like it, from all I've heard. Buck up. How about a nice game of checkers?" he added, in the voice of a man who says good morning without expecting an answer.

Lennie staggered him by saying "Why not?" and winning hands down.

ELEVEN

For all his buoyancy Crook's face was as grave as a churchyard as he remounted the Old Superb and shot back to Burtonwood. It grew darker yet in the days that followed. Every lead seemed to be an arrow pointing nowhere. Bill had been to Somerset House but there was no record of their Sidney Mount having contracted a marriage prior to 1938. In this year he had married Else Huerter, widow of Johann Huerter, in front of the British Consul in Berlin. On the register Mount was described as a bachelor. At this stage it was useless to hope they could learn anything fresh from Germany. The whole of the country had been turned upside down since then. Nevertheless, Crook stuck to his guns that Mount's trouble had something to do with those prewar years. And events were to prove him right.

His one hope now was Harries, but the line from Elsham seemed to have gone dead. Either Mount's visitor had got wind of danger or he was withholding his hand for reasons of his own. Harries watched like a cat at a mousehole with nary a smell of a mouse. Several days passed. Crook went back to London; Dinah James ate her heart out in Burtonwood. Lennie steadily played checkers and practically always won.

Crook knew a sense of desperation. There was a

bare week left, and still he could assemble no facts sufficiently strong to ask for a stay of execution. Then suddenly everything happened at once. He had been out of London for a night on a job that had nothing to do with Lennie Hunter and returned to the office to find Bill agog.

"What's up?" he demanded. "Never seen your temperature up a point in twenty years."

"Harries has come through with the goods at last," said Bill. And told the story in his own words.

It appeared that the mysterious visitor had surfaced again when they had almost abandoned hope of his doing so in time to be of any use to Lennie Hunter. He had driven up to the Ring o' Bells in a handsome black car and gone into the restaurant. A minute or two later Mount appeared, coming on foot, and followed very discreetly by Harries. The pair had taken a table and Harries had managed to get a small one close by.

"According to him, this chap, who spoke with a foreign accent, had the pants scared off Mount. He looked like death."

"His own or someone else's?" wondered Crook.

"Harries couldn't hear much, the place was pretty full and he was some tables away, but he does lip reading as you know and it was obvious that this chap was pressing Mount pretty hard. Mount was asking for time. This chap said, more or less, 'Time, time, that is always your answer. When the old woman died you said now everything would be all right.' "

"What was Mount's comeback to that?"

"Something about it not being in his—the stranger's

—interest to push him too hard. X said, 'Perhaps I should approach Mrs. Mount.' That really sent the balloon up. Mount said—Harries is quite sure of this— 'If you try to speak to her I shall murder you.' The other chap laughed. Harries said it chilled his blood to hear him. 'You must know by now, you of all people, that murder pays no dividend. If I were to tell what I know . . .' Mount, who seemed to have gone completely around the bend by this time, said, 'You will never do that. So much I promise you.' Talk about crime drama," added Bill.

"Just at the moment we're talking about Sidney Mount," suggested Crook, pleasantly. "Did Harries get any hint who this chap was?"

"He says he followed him back to the garage at Finney's Bridge—it was a hired car and I suppose he didn't care about public transport or couldn't get on— it was Market Day in Elsham—and then X made for the station. Harries admits he blundered there. He should have parked his car and gone on foot. Because there was a traffic jam and he got held up while a policeman sorted it out and by the time he reached the station the London train was just drawing out with, of course, our boy on it. However, he didn't do too badly . . . He hung about for a while and then went back to the garage and said his friend had just left a car—he was able to give the number—and he thought he'd dropped a scarf between the front seats. He'd had to get back on the London train, but he'd asked Harries to take a look. It so happened the car had just gone out again, but the proprietor said very civilly he'd ask when it was brought back and if the scarf was there he'd mail it on. Harries asked if he'd got the chap's address, and he turned up a book and said, 'Yes, 29 Barkis Street, S.W.9. The name was Kleiner.' Harries stopped at Elsham, partly to keep an eye on Mount and partly because he thought he might be recognized if he went tailing Kleiner, who looks the sort of chap who doesn't stop at anything, and Mrs. Harries thinks her Joe's too young to die."

"Anyway we want him," said Crook, absorbedly. "Got the info on 29 Barkis Street?"

"It's a sort of boarding house—mainly foreigners. I got the telephone number and asked for Kleiner but he was out. Still there's no talk of his leaving in a hurry. He's been there since the summer . . ."

"About the time the trouble began," said Crook, consideringly. "I've never believed Mount took that brooch back because he wanted to save the insurance; he went because he had to see his auntie. Well, perhaps we can get going at last. There's times," he added almost wistfully, "when I find myself agreeing with our Mr. Mount. Some murders do seem justified. You might see if you can get a line on Kleiner, Bill. Me, I'm for Burtonwood at crack of dawn." He moved across to the window. "Second thoughts," he suggested, "it might be best to go down right away. I don't like the look of that sky. It spells snow to me."

Bill said nothing. Crook had been driving since dawn but fatigue was something he couldn't have spelled. "Anything else turned up I ought to know about?" he asked. "Apart from Mount, I mean?"

Bill told him. Crook nodded. "Well, you can handle that lot, can't you? I'll call through tonight, and if there are any developments this end you do likewise."

He hadn't gone above a few miles when the snow began to fall, coming down at first in pretty twirling flakes that melted as they touched the ground. But he had been no more than an hour on the road before he knew his good sense had served him well once again. At this rate there wouldn't be any motoring tomorrow, and he thought of his car as a part of himself. Crook traveling by train wasn't half the man Crook was when he came down in the Superb. The storm increased in violence with every mile and a journey that should have taken two hours and a half took just twice that time. Before he reached Elsham he had come upon cars stranded by the roadside with the snow up to their mudguards. The snow plows would be out before morning in the valleys and unless the downfall abated Operation Snowdrop would be put in force for remote villages in Scotland and the wilder parts of England.

The speed and ferocity of the storm made him think of an air raid when in a few hours the whole face of a familiar environment could become unrecognizable. He had a sixth sense for direction, but even so he missed his road twice. Once he had to stop at a gas pump for a refill and the man who came out cheerfully enough, for customers that day were few, made the idiotic remark, 'Pretty, ain't it? Like a Christmas card.'

"Whited sepulcher," retorted Crook, who was devoid of all poetical sense. "You'll see, tomorrow we

shall hear of chaps stranded on Helvellyn or somewhere and other chaps will risk their lives going up to
fetch 'em down. Amateurs!" He snorted.

"No one makes 'em go climbing that I can see," said
the man, bringing a rag and wiping the windshield.
"No sense blaming the snow if they do get lost."

"Well, then, how about sheep?" demanded Crook.

His companion admitted that sheep were different.
The snow was tough on them.

Crook paid his bill and drove on; necessarily he
made a slow pace; the darkness came down much too
early, and at one time he guided himself by the lights
in the nearest cottages and farm dwellings. He thought
nostalgically of London, where the wheels of the endless traffic would have churned the snow into a brown
revolting slush. "London," he thought tenderly. "My
home town. Noisy?" he'd say indignantly to those
who spoke of noise and smells, "what about your per-
ishing birds?" Once he heard a church clock striking
and slowed up to count the strokes. He was shocked
to discover it was already five o'clock and there was
still a night's work to be done. He reached Burtonwood about six but he daren't stop for a quick one and
a chance to book a room for the night. He could call
from Elsham, which was his immediate goal. It was
nearly an hour later when he sited the town and drew
up at the pub where Harries was staying.

Harries came to meet him. "My goodness, Mr.
Crook, I didn't think you'd get through," he said.
"Parsons telephoned to expect you. Chaps coming in
are full of tales of travelers stranded on the roads, and

the electricity's gone at Heybourne ten miles away. Lines for candles, they say, and the stock exhausted already. Tom Primer's congratulating himself for once on making his own electricity."

"Let's hope it don't last long," said Crook, plunging his grateful face into a tankard of beer. "Anything new to report?"

Harries shook his head. "Only thing I thought of was Mount putting his head in the gas oven, but I hear the gas supply's down to a trickle, so he can't take that way out, and if he jumps out of the window he'll simply fall into a snowbank."

"You must be a great comfort to your wife," said Crook. "Come on, I'm going to send a telegram. I want Kleiner down here and I want him fast."

"You won't get through to London tonight, sir," said the landlord. "Lines are all down thanks to the snow. Kings Proctor's the nearest town that was still operating an hour ago, and they may be down there by this time."

"How far's Kings Proctor?" asked Crook.

"Matter of five-and-twenty miles. You're never thinking of trying to get there tonight, surely. It's a narrow road and it's got one of those breakneck hills. You could go over the edge and no one 'ud be any the wiser till the thaw."

Crook drummed his fingers on the counter. "How about the mail trains? I suppose they'll go through."

The landlord glanced at the clock on the wall. "You've missed the mail for today," he said. "Goes out at six-thirty everywhere hereabouts, and they're quick about clearing the boxes at any time."

Something clicked in Crook's brain. His face looked oddly pale under his flaming red thatch.

"Must be an express service or something," he urged.

"This isn't London," said the landlord, smiling.

Crook's scowl was as dark as the sky. "You're telling me," he said.

He bought another round and then got back to the Superb. "No, don't tell me I can't get through," he implored. "It's a matter of life and death. I've got to make Burtonwood tonight, if I walk every step of the way."

It seemed as if he might even have to do that, and a car of less gallant heart than the Superb could never have stood up to that journey. It was a matter of fifteen miles and normally he'd have taken her through in twenty minutes at most; it was an unbuilt-up area the greater part of the way. Tonight it took him an hour, and he felt dead to the world as he stumbled into the bar of the Seven Moons. He was greeted with complimentary warmth by George Pigott.

"You've never brought her down from London in this, Mr. Crook?"

"Well, I didn't fly," said Crook, quite grumpily for him.

Pigott sent him a careful glance. "Things moving?" he ventured.

"Say it," said Crook. "I'm daffy, off my rocker. I

couldn't agree with you more. Mucking around, with the facts staring me in the face. I suppose your telephone wires are down, too?" he added. "Here, what's this stuff you've given me?"

"Rum and ginger wine, Mr. Crook. Best thing to keep out the cold. Yes, they came down some hours ago."

"And I suppose your mail goes out six-thirty, too? All right, so I can't contact London till the wires are restored."

"They won't lose any time," Pigott told him in the cheerful tone of one to whom a telephone is nothing but a nuisance. "You can have the same room as you had last time, Mr. Crook, and the water's piping hot. We don't depend on gas at the Seven Moons," he added, rather smugly.

"That'll be good for when I get back," Crook told him.

George stared. "You're never going out again in this?"

"I've wasted time enough as it is. Shan't be long, though."

"Walking?"

"I'll be wanting the Superb tomorrow if all goes well, next day anyhow. I don't want to have to walk out to a snowdrift to collect her. Mind you, I've always said that if Providence had meant us to be pedestrians we'd have been given four feet same as the beasts. Seeing we only have two, it's pretty clear to me why. One for the brake, one for the accelerator.

Still, count your blessings. Mine are pretty solid specimens." He looked down with momentary satisfaction at his own enormous beetle-crushers in bright tan Oxfords. "If I'm not back in an hour send out a search party," he suggested. "And don't forget the dog with the keg around its neck."

The snow, that had started so suddenly, was already thinning and would have stopped before midnight. He was away no more than twenty minutes and later ate a Gargantuan meal that made even the experienced Pigott draw a respectful breath. Then, having seen to it that the Superb was comfortably bedded down for the night, he turned in himself and slept like a log. One of his favorite quotations was 'Sufficient unto the day is the evil thereof.' And if his guess was right there'd be plenty more where that came from in the morning.

Dinah James might look like a flower, as more than one man had assured her, but she was as tough as a little pony, and a fall of snow wasn't going to keep her indoors. It was too dark to go sliding, of course, but anything was better than sitting in a solitary room and thinking about Lennie, so she put a woolen tasseled hood over her butter-bright hair and took herself to the local movie. When she came back she found an envelope addressed to herself on the mat of the house where she lived. The handwriting was unfamiliar. She opened it under the meager hall light and found two scrawled lines on the single sheet within.

"Find out what time Kate Winter went
out on the night Emily Foss died."

She stood staring, the chilled blood slowly heating
till her face burned; excitement shook her from head
to foot. She didn't stop to ask why Mr. Crook wanted
to know, she only thought, "He doesn't do anything
for fun. We've rounded the corner at last."

She stood there tongue-tied and exultant, until the
landlady poked her head around the corner of the
stairs and asked what was wrong.

"Not frozen to a stachoo, I hope?" she said.

Dinah looked at her as if she were something from
the prehistoric world; then she folded the bit of paper
and went up to bed.

Patience is a virtue,
Virtue is a grace.
Put them both together
And they make your pretty face.

Mr. Crook's Sunday school teacher had recited this
jingle to her class half a century before.

"Can't be meant for me," Crook had decided, after
a glance in the mirror, and promptly forgot it. But
life had been teaching him the same lesson ever since.

Next morning the snow had stopped altogether and
the barometer rose a little. The papers were full of
hard luck stories about the effects of the storm, and,
as he had prophesied, certain remote places were al-

ready snowbound and waiting for help from the outside world. There was no likelihood of a thaw before midday, but Pigott assured him that the men from the telephone service were already getting to work. "Be able to talk to London again tonight I shouldn't wonder," he said.

Crook prowled like a lion in a too-small cage for the rest of the morning. There was nothing he could do, and he'd never been much of a reader. "One of the things I'm keeping for when I retire," he used to explain. He could do nothing till he heard from Dinah James.

He had to wait till six o'clock, and then she brought her answer in person.

"I'm sorry I couldn't make it before," she said apologetically. "But the telephone's only just working, and Kate Winter's like the eye that never sleeps. Besides, it wasn't as easy as all that to bring the subject up. I had to tell her at last that you were back. Was it all right?"

"She was bound to find out," Crook agreed, accepting as simple fact that he was the sort of person you couldn't easily overlook. "What did she say?"

"She went out at four o'clock that afternoon, seeing Mr. Bastable wouldn't be wanting any supper. But she said she didn't desert her post in the ordinary way. That was one for me, in case I asked if I could get off early one day. Not that I would. There'd be no sense. There's nothing I can do, since Lennie won't see me."

"Didn't drop a hint when she got back, I suppose?"

"Oh, quite late. It's the most extraordinary thing. If only the luck had been a bit different she might have stood surety for Lennie that night."

"How come?" asked Crook.

"She was at the Roxy, too."

"That what she told you?"

"Yes. Why shouldn't she have been?"

"Well, I suppose she had to be somewhere," Crook agreed. "Go to the same house?"

"Yes. She went to have tea with a friend who's somebody else's housekeeper. Her employer was going to the Marks' party too. Kate seemed quite put out about it. 'You'd think if people had to have parties they might consider other people's convenience,' she said. 'Friday's late closing night here, all the shops stay open till seven. Not Miss Foss,' she added, 'but the food shops and some of the dress shops. It makes it easier for the housewives on Saturday if they can do some of their shopping the night before.' Kate said she always did the worst of the shopping on Friday. She doesn't hold with standing in lines—'all right for Londoners, no doubt,' she says, 'and fly-by-nights'— by which she means people who've only settled here since the war—but she's lived hereabouts for forty years and she thinks that ought to give her priority. She always shops at Marks', but of course on Friday she couldn't, so she had to walk right up the town to Knight's, where she says nothing's quite so good and they're insolent if you're not a regular customer."

"Let's get this straight," said Crook. "She went out

to tea, and then she did some shopping—take it home before going to the pictures?"

"No. That was one of her grouses. Marks sends everything, of course, but Knight's won't. She had to carry everything in a big string bag, and some clod in the movies kicked it and smashed a bottle of something. Mr. Crook, what does it all mean?"

"Didn't they ever teach you arithmetic at your school?" Crook demanded. "Not that I'm one to talk. I daresay she made quite a to-do about her busted bottle."

"I should think so," agreed the girl, fervently.

"So they'd remember her being there. Let's see, the picture started about six, didn't it?"

"Yes. She left her friend's house about six and said she'd meet her at the pictures. A silly piece, she told me. I don't know whether she meant the friend or the picture. Mr. Crook, does that help?"

"Sure it helps," said Crook, heartily. "I don't know what I'd do without you and that's a fact. Or Lennie either, for that matter. Now listen to what you're to do and don't ask any questions. I'll give you all the details later."

When she heard what he wanted of her she just stared. "But—there's nothing in that," she protested. "I don't understand."

"You will. Now just do as I say. And remember, it gets cold of an evening. Put on an extra scarf. Don't want to have you dying of pneumonia or anything else before this case is finished."

TWELVE

It took Crook nearly two hours to get his London call, there were so many priorities held up from the day before. Soon after eight-thirty he heard Bill's cool voice at the other end of the phone.

"Get cracking," said Crook. "Want you to pay a visit to a firm in the City in the morning." He supplied the address. "See what you can get out of them and let me have it pronto. If it turns out the way I expect, we're at journey's end pretty nearly. Me, I'm going over to Elsham in the morning to pull in Mount, poor devil. All bein' well—from our point of view, that is—the curtain rises on the last act tomorrow night."

They wouldn't let him talk for more than three minutes, too much pressure on the lines, and he hadn't anything else to say anyhow.

The bar that evening was pretty full. Bastable came in about nine o'clock. He looked a bit put out.

"What's the idea, this girl of yours upsetting Kate?" he demanded.

So Dinah hadn't been as clever as she thought. "Didn't know she had?" returned Mr. Crook, blandly. "What's yours?"

"Trying to find out how she spent the evening Emily Foss was attacked—I don't get it. How can Kate come into the picture?"

"Picture's the operative word. It seems she was at the Roxy that night, same house as Master Hunter."

"If he was there," corrected Bastable. "Well, but she can't hope Kate's going to come forward at this stage and say she saw him."

"She wouldn't be believed if she did, but you know what girls are. Grab at straws."

"Even a girl like that, as mad as a hatter—well, she must be to think she can do anything now—can't imagine Kate was involved."

"She's told me she'd involve the Archbishop of Canterbury if she thought it would help."

"As likely suggest one as the other," offered Bastable. Crook looked at him reflectively. "Did you know Emily Foss was threatening Kate with the sack?"

"If she did she was screwy. Don't know what I'd do without Kate. Look here, have you got anything up your sleeve besides your arm?"

"Oh, I'm like Dinah James," confessed Crook, candidly. "I'd involve His Grace if it would do us any good. By the way, there ain't any truth in the idea, I suppose, that you were giving Kate the air?"

"Of course not. I've just told you—I couldn't do without her. What are you thinking?" he added, suspiciously.

"When I talked to her, first time around, she said a thing that might mean something or might not. 'Most of us have something in our past we wouldn't want broadcasted . . .' That was the meaning of it, if it wasn't the exact words. Ring a bell with you?"

"If you mean, do I know anything discreditable

about Kate, the answer's no." Bastable seemed absolutely flabbergasted, knocked all of a heap.

"How much do you know about her?"

Bastable considered. "Not a lot really, I suppose. She came to me with a perfectly respectable reference when I settled here, and it wasn't too easy to find suitable women then—no easier now, I daresay. If she hadn't wanted to stay she could have got another job any time. Look here, you're not suggesting any funny business between her and me . . . ?"

"My dear chap, of course not. In that case Miss Foss would have proceeded against you—laying out info, I mean—if she was fool enough to poke her nose in at all. No, but—any notion of Kate's private life before she became your housekeeper?"

"It's not my concern," said Bastable, shortly. "But I can tell you this, I've never heard a word against her."

"But then your name ain't Paul Pry," Crook reminded him. "Miss Foss was different. And it's no secret there was no love lost between the pair of them."

"I suppose this is your girl's idea," said Bastable sharply. "She'd rake over a muck heap for evidence if she thought there was a chance of finding it there."

"Or forge it, if she knew how. And I, for one, don't blame her. And I wouldn't dismiss her too lightly, if I were you. It's my belief she's on to something."

"She can't be."

"Well, we'll know tomorrow night. If she can get the missing link, it'll be a case of the open road for Lennie Hunter. If she can't—but we won't think about that."

"Where on earth does she think she's going to find it?"

"Oh, not a hundred miles from here," said Crook. "Look, my dear fellow, don't ride me now. Come to the unmasking tomorrow night, if you'd care to. At six in this very pub. George is going to let me have a private room. It'll be worth it," he added, dryly. "We're having everyone in, everyone concerned, that is."

"Including the nephew?"

"Yes. I must issue him an invitation. After all, he's been in this from the start. He's going to have a bit of a shock, but that's the way things happen in our line. By the way, if young Dinah wants to get off early tomorrow, tell Kate that's O.K. by you. She's doing a little chore for me on her way here."

"I wish you wouldn't be so damned mysterious." Bastable sounded perturbed. "Crook, you're a good chap. I hate to see you make a fool of yourself. I swear you're barking up the wrong tree if you've got Kate in your eye."

"Let's put it this way," conceded Crook. "I believe Kate could give us enough data to get Lennie Hunter off the rope. That's all I have to do. I don't have to replace him, though of course it does happen that way sometimes. And are the police grateful? Stop me on the street and ask me."

"Any objection to my telling Kate what you're after?" Bastable demanded.

"I leave that to you. Look here"—even Mr. Crook seemed less than his normal smooth self—"this ain't all jam for me. And now we've got to a pitch where I can't control the march of events. It all depends on the girl—and on information I'm waiting for from another quarter, I've got to use shock tactics now— the choice is out of my hands—and it could be more than one person's going to get a shock. And that's all I can tell you till tomorrow night at six P.M."

When Bastable reached home his housekeeper had already gone to bed. He poured himself a final whiskey and soda from the decanter she always left ready for him and while he drank it he brooded over what he had heard tonight. He was in a state of complete be-fuddlement. What on earth had given Crook the idea that Kate might be involved?

"It's not possible," he said aloud. Crook was a wily old bird, looked as open as a spring morning, but he knew how to keep his big mouth shut. And Dinah James? What could she conceivably be going to learn? He decided to tell Kate to let the girl go early if she wanted to. She'd take French leave if she wasn't given it, he decided wryly. He returned to his thought of Kate. In the twelve years she had served him he had never really thought of her as a person with a private life of her own. She might have been married, had an illegitimate child, forged a will, poisoned an old lady, anything, he didn't know. She looked after him com-petently enough, and if she had an arrangement with the shops, well, where was the harm? She kept the books and showed them to him every month, though he never gave them more than the most cursory glance. A single man is always in demand and he dined out as often as he dined at home. Kate had plenty of spare time, was free to go out any evening he didn't require her. Was she running a secret affair and Emily had stumbled on it and was threatening to broadcast it? Precisely what Emily would do, he had to admit. No, if Emily had been uttering threats the odds were she'd discovered something discreditable in the past; she was quite capable of it, she bored away like a mole.

Next morning at breakfast he couldn't forebear to say, "Have you heard the latest, Kate? Mr. Crook's about to solve our local mystery?"

She didn't turn a hair; her face was as scornful as always when Crook's name was mentioned.

"Can't think why he bothers. That young chap hasn't got a penny nor has the girl. Why can't he leave things to the police? It's their job, isn't it?"

"He doesn't seem to agree with the police."

"All these Nosy Parkers," said Kate, pushing a rack of toast onto the table. "Going around asking questions and trying to ferret things out."

That shook him a bit. "Such as?"

"Oh, I don't know. I haven't any patience with him. He wants to look out he doesn't go the same way as Emily Foss. That girl seems to have got him in her pocket."

"Oh yes. Dinah James. If she asks if she can go off early today, Kate, don't stop her. She's going to get our Mr. Crook his final proof."

"And where's she going to find that?"

"I didn't ask, but I'll be able to tell you this evening. There's going to be a grand finale at the Seven Moons at six P.M., and I've got an invitation. Think of coming along?" he added.

"I've got better things to do with my time. As for the girl, we shan't be wanting her after this week anyway. Mrs. Raymond's coming back Monday, and I must say I shan't be sorry to see her. Give me a sensible middle-aged woman any day rather than one of these young flibbertigibbets."

"She's a treat to look at," said Bastable, rashly. "Like a hummingbird."

"The proper place for hummingbirds is a jungle or the zoo." The housekeeper refused to be placated.

"Why have you got your knife into her?" asked Bastable, curiously. "She seems a nice girl."

"If she was a nice girl she wouldn't be mixed up with that young Hunter. But they're all the same these days, as wild as Shetland ponies. As for that Mr. Crook, he seems to have upset everyone. Nothing's like it used to be. I'll be glad when he goes back to London."

He wondered why she said that. Crook hadn't bothered her much. It couldn't be because she was in any way involved with Emily Foss's death. They didn't speak of the subject again. She asked if he would be in to lunch and he said yes, but she could get off any time she liked in the afternoon. It wasn't a busy morning at the office, and he had plenty of time to brood. He found himself thinking continuously about what the night would bring.

He would have been surprised to know that Crook also was like a cat on hot bricks. When he looked out of his window the evening before The Day he saw that, though the snow might have stopped falling, a thick white blanket cloaked the countryside. During the night he woke once or twice to hear a dull thud as a great lump of the stuff fell from a tree and crashed on to his window sill; and when he rose the next day the world still presented a white appearance. A keen wind had sprung up and iced over the snow, which glittered brilliantly in the frosty sunshine. As the chap at the filling station had remarked, it was all as pretty as a Christmas card, and as far removed as possible from thoughts of murder and hatred and deeds executed in the deadly dark.

All morning he hung about waiting for a call from Bill, but it was twelve-thirty before it came through.

"Your guess was right," said Bill, never one to waste words. "No communication at all."

"Not in any direction?"

"One letter shortly before the old lady died."

"You've taken a weight off my mind," Crook confessed. "I was following a hunch and it might have landed me in a bog. Well, all's over now bar the hanging and for once I shan't be sorry. The fact is, I'm getting too old to be hustled. I like to do things in a seemly manner. All this ain't up my street at all."

Bill prudently held his tongue. The police of the entire Metropolitan area would have laughed to hear that.

Putting down the telephone Crook went into the bar for a snack before taking the car into Elsham. On the way he stopped at a post office to send a telegram. It was addressed to: Kleiner, 29 Barkis Street, S.W.9., and read:

> "Meet me Seven Moons Burtonwood tonight
> six P.M. Most urgent. Don't telephone."

He signed it Mount.

Twenty minutes later he pulled up at the jeweler's shop in Elsham and invited the proprietor to spare him five minutes.

"You can have the lady in on this if you like," he offered, but Mount said sharply that his wife was out with friends. He could not say when she would return. Crook wasn't sure if he believed that.

"I'm considering sending her away for a holiday," Mount added. "I can't have her scared out of her wits every time you feel like paying a call."

"This is the last time," Crook promised. "All is done, or will be by six P.M. tonight. That's why I'm over here, to suggest that you join the meeting at the Seven Moons."

"Why should I?" demanded Mount.

"Up to you," agreed Crook, "but you might like to be there to put in a word on your own behalf, explain when a murder isn't a murder, for instance."

"You like talking in riddles, I see," Mount commented.

"Well, not really," Crook apologized. "I'm known as the Plain Man of the Law List."

"Who else is going to be at this surprise party of yours?"

"Oh, just a few local people—and a chap called Kleiner. Coming down from London on purpose."

He thought for a moment Mount would drop where he stood.

"What devil's trick is this? What's Kleiner to do with the affair?"

"As if you didn't know!"

"You've been spying on me, I see."

"You didn't give me any choice. I like a straight road as well as any man, but when you put up your roadblocks, then I have to take the detour."

"Did it ever occur to you how astounding it is that you've lived so long?" inquired Mount, bitterly.

"I know the answer. Because so far I've always managed to be one jump ahead of the other chap. One day my joints'll stiffen and then it'll be his turn, but I don't mean that to happen tomorrow night. Not that I'm in any special danger. I've seen to that. It's little Dinah James who's in the key spot. There's a girl for you. If she lets me down we're sunk, because if I don't get my last bit of evidence I've no case at all. But somehow I don't think she will—let me down, I mean. Got too much on the ball."

"You don't mind risking everyone else's life, I note," Mount taunted him.

"The life I'm engaged to save is Lennie Hunter's. Of course it's bound to be a risk to someone else, but I didn't make the circumstances. As I said, you don't have to come, but I rather think you will." Succinctly he told him why.

Mount heard him out, then he said, white-lipped, "It's infamous. If the police adopted your tactics there'd be questions asked in the House."

"The police do things their own way, and the result is Lennie Hunter in clink. My job, and my only job start to finish—and I've said this till my tongue's tired —is to get him out of prison. Everyone else has got to take his chance, you included. Well, do we see you or not?"

"I'll come," agreed Mount. "Mind you, I think your action's indefensible, but the way you put it I haven't any choice."

"No," agreed Crook, gently, "somehow I thought you'd see it that way."

All the same, when he was making his way back, Crook didn't look as pleased as you might have anticipated. "Come another war," he told himself, "I should join the espionage gang. Judas Iscariot Crook, who opens wide his smiling jaws to welcome fishes in." He was taking an almighty risk and he knew it, and this time it wasn't just his own life he was chucking in the balance. True, the snare was well and truly set, but— how to make certain the right bird would spring it? "The fact is," he told himself, "I'm getting old. I don't like being hustled, only there's no time to do things in a proper and seemly way." He took a corner on two wheels. It was proof of his nervous state and would have startled Bill, to whom a case was just a case and all the people concerned as cardboard as actors on the stage. Murder was wrong, of course, but some murderers asked for it, and the ensuing bill generally took everything you'd got.

"Oh, stop bein' Little Lord Fauntleroy," he told himself impatiently, taking another corner at a speed that nearly caused an elderly lady to fall off her bicycle. "You owe young Hunter something, don't you?"

It was typical of the gap in his logic that he didn't stop to wonder what.

THIRTEEN

The worst part of a battle is when you are waiting to go over the top. Crook seldom thought of his war days, now so far behind him, but for some reason this evening the memories came crowding back. He recalled a boy in the trenches in 1917 who had almost succumbed to hysteria, had tried to crawl out on his own. "I can't stand the suspense," he had whispered. Crook had knocked sense into him in the most elementary fashion and lived to see him get the Military Medal. He hadn't suffered from nerves in those days, didn't often suffer now, but this evening was the exception. "Fact is, I should be thinking about my retirement pension," he told himself, and then was comforted to realize that there were still several years before he could claim it. This anxiety aged a man as no vigorous set-to did. At half past five he ordered and consumed a large whiskey, a drink for which as a rule he had no use at all. At five-forty he was ready for the show to start. With the exception of Kate Winter, he expected them all in the next twenty minutes.

At five-forty-five the telephone rang and George went to answer it. Crook began to shrug himself into his heavy checked overcoat.

"It's for you, Mr. Crook," called George.

"Say I'm dead, say anything you like. I can't stop. Who is it, anyway?"

"I'll ask. It's Mr. Bastable," he reported an instant later.

"Bastable?"

"Yes. Says he can't come tonight, after all. He's been poisoned or something. Wants a word with you."

Crook stood like an enormous snowman, his muffler half covering his big red face. "Poisoned?" he repeated. "George, shut off for a minute or two. Then call through again and say you find I've gone out, but I'll be seeing him later."

"Murderers," he reflected as he hurried over the road to the Common, "are either plain dumb or else as wily as serpents." This time he was dealing with the wily sort.

"Poisoned," he said to himself, stamping into the untrodden snow. "That's a new one. I hadn't expected that."

Everything now depended on perfect timing to avoid the second murder he was resolved should not take place. He was shocked to find he was less steady than usual; all of a shake, in fact. He stopped a minute to complete his plans. He wasn't going to be the only chap on the Common that night, no matter how reluctant the others might be.

The Common seemed much wider and more eerie than usual in the dark blue wintry light. Anyone crossing it would be no more than a speck among the trees and the clumps of bramble and gorse. As he set forth the snow began to fall again, getting in his eyes, half blinding him.

At five-forty-five Mount left his car at the farther end of the Common under a big oak, and walked out of the shadow. His gaunt figure, in dark clothes to match the occasion, was almost invisible as he hesitated beside the wall of a house fronting the Green. For him time stood still, though his heart raced hard enough. Like Crook, he knew this evening spelled for him the parting of the ways and heaven only knew how it was going to end. And he, too, shivered, at the thought of the night's work.

At five-fifty Dinah James appeared at the end of a long road and in her turn made her way toward the snow-covered Common. She passed so close to Mount that he could have touched her by putting out his hand, but it was too soon—too soon. He let her go ahead for a few paces, then stole softly in her wake. If she looked around he could rely on the snow to conceal his identity, if not his actual presence, and anyway he was skilled in the art of camouflage; it was an art he had learned overseas when an ability to become part of the landscape could make the whole difference between life and death.

A minute or two later there came from the farther side of the Common another figure, so wrapped in a thick coat and scarf, so humped against the windblown snow, it was impossible in that wretched light to tell if it were man or woman. This figure began to cross the Common in a diagonal direction; Mount drew back farther under the trees, seemed to melt into them, and proceeded on his way, his eyes fixed on the hurrying girl.

Always he let her stay a little ahead, but not far, not far; then, smooth as a snake and still keeping in the shadow of the welcome trees, he would draw near again. On the wet snow-covered grass his rubber-shod feet made no sound. The clumps of bush and brier with which the Common was dotted made it easy for a man of his experience to disappear at the first hint of danger. But she never once looked around. The only light came from the lamps set along the Common's verge and these did little to illuminate the path. Even the snow looked dark under the dark, unfriendly sky.

Dinah James thrust her hands into the pockets of her coat and wound her scarf more closely about her throat. It took no more than seven or eight minutes to reach the security of the lighted inn, where Crook would be waiting for her, to give Lennie Hunter's life into her hands. She didn't argue how or why. He had said it would be all right, and she clung to that promise as men threatened with drowning cling to a rope.

She saw nothing of Mr. Crook, a little black figure fighting through the snow, and she wasn't as yet aware of the other figure coming, like herself, to keep a ghastly rendezvous.

At the lighted door of the Seven Moons George stood whistling softly. "What a caper," he was thinking. Better than the pictures, and a whole lot better than that silly television his wife was always after him to install. After a minute or two he remembered the mission with which Crook had charged him and went back to ring Bastable's house. But though he could hear the bell shrilling away, and he waited all of two minutes in case the poor chap was in the bathroom being sick or something, there was no reply.

Something Crook had said repeated itself over and over in the girl's mind as she made steadily for the lights of the Seven Moons. "One foot in front of the other, one foot in front of the other, and so to the top of the mountain." For the first time since Crook had undertaken the case she was conscious of deathly fear. Darkness was no stranger to her—it couldn't be that—she was accustomed to work at all hours, though, like Crook, she longed for the friendly lights and sounds of London. A bird whirred past uttering a strange cry, making her think of Poe's old phony, the raven, with his idiot prophecy—"Nevermore, nevermore." She shook herself angrily. Only a pigeon or something most likely. She didn't know about birds. Robins, of course, and sparrows, and ducks on a pond, but nothing else. The countryside seemed full of birds who were as strange and inimicable as this endless night. But she turned her thoughts away from herself and concentrated on Lennie, whose life depended on this evening's work, though she didn't understand how she was helping simply by walking across the Common to keep a rendezvous at the Seven Moons.

She had accomplished half her journey when she heard the following feet, coming up behind her. "Don't look around," she counseled herself. "Don't panic. Whatever you do, don't run." Another two minutes—or three—appalling to reflect what a single minute could achieve.

"You're all right, all right, all right," she told herself; and suddenly remembered Emily Foss marching into the Court, the coppers in her hand. She must have thought she was all right, too.

Suddenly an unwary step caused her to slip and founder in the treacherous path and, as though that were a signal, the feet came on at a run. Now at last she did turn her head, but it was too late; her enemy's face was obscured from her by hat and scarf drawn over eyes and jaw. Now hands had caught the ends of the heavy scarf she had donned at Crook's request, were drawing it tight, tighter, a weight was pushing her down, she felt alien breath on her cheek. Now, too late, she tried to cry out, but her voice was suffocated in her throat. The sky whirled, trees seemed suddenly up-ended, flying into the dark; her hands, fighting those ruthless hands, were like straw or the fingers of a baby. Last of all she tried to call Crook's name, but even that husky whisper was smothered in the immensity of enveloping night.

A light flared suddenly, blinding her, causing her antagonist's frantic hold to relax at last. Big hands caught her, pulling her erect. Crook's voice said,

"O.K., honey, that's fine. Just lean on your Uncle Arthur. I only hope that boy of yours knows what he's getting."

"Talk about the Hound of Heaven," he was thinking. "Why, Lennie Hunter never stood a chance from the start. A girl like this would never let him go."

She felt all virtue ooze out of her; her legs trembled, all her courage seemed to dissipate in the cold air.

"Hold it, sugar," Crook implored. "I know women enjoy a good cry, but wait till we're under cover, and I'll send you a box of the best handkerchiefs, gold-edged. I wouldn't call myself a timid man," he added, "but I understand why chaps flinched from the Amazons. Why, they'd make me run a mile."

As breath began to come more evenly, she straightened and looked about her. People seemed to have sprung up from every side, but actually there were only four there besides herself. The light came from a policeman's lantern; it shone on the tall shaking figure of Sidney Mount, speechless and pale, and the short alert one of Arthur Bastable, the two men standing so close they might have been Siamese twins.

"Very nice, Bastable," said Crook. "Couldn't have done it better if it had been rehearsed. Mind you, I wouldn't have objected to a rehearsal. It was touch and go, and you can't think what a job I had persuading the police to aid and abet me in a second near-murder. That's the way the old lady was killed, isn't it?"

His bright brown eyes swept the little group about him. Mount tried to speak, but the words wouldn't come.

"That's O.K.," said Crook. "You'll have time enough. We're all going along to the station. There's an escort waiting for us just over there. We're important people, ain't we, officer?"

Bastable said something about madness, staring at the girl's pale working face.

"Murder's generally mad," Crook agreed, "only not within the meanin' of the Act. Oh, we're going to get a true-blue verdict this time, or my name ain't Arthur Crook. O.K., officer, do your stuff."

The police sergeant said in a wooden sort of voice ("even when I come to the assistance of the police they're never grateful," Crook would complain), "Arthur Bastable, you are under arrest for the attempted murder of Dinah James. You are not required to make a statement, but . . ."

Bastable turned, but before he could move Mount had got him in a grip that nearly dislocated his collarbone. The other police, at a signal, came across the grass, and Bastable went away walking between them. They hadn't even forgotten the handcuffs upon his wrists.

The police having waived the official visit till a more convenient time, the other three walked very slowly toward the Seven Moons, the girl between the two men. No one spoke. Mount was thinking of Kleiner; Crook was sorting his ideas preparatory to the statement he'd have to make; Dinah, of course, thought only of Lennie. Already she could put out of mind the vicious attack upon herself.

As they came into the pub George Pigott caught

Crook's eye and indicated a private room on the left of the bar. He leaned over as Crook came by.

"I rang Mr. Bastable again," he confided. "Wasn't any answer. Didn't know if I should ring a doctor, but I suppose Kate's there."

"That's O.K.," said Crook. "He's being looked after. Anyone been asking for Mr. Mount? No? When and if so, show him into the private room."

"What made you invite him?" muttered Mount. Dinah had slipped off to tidy herself after her encounter.

"No harm letting him see you've got a lawyer. Mightn't be so anxious to keep up the acquaintance once he knows."

"It's you who don't know," said Mount, desperately.

"Only yourself to thank if that's true. And you can't blame me if I thought for a while it was you who put out your auntie's light. You had me properly foxed, talking about murder, and then Kleiner coming down and doing likewise, and you not giving him a black eye or even saying no. Fact is, it didn't occur to me at first we could be talking about different murders."

Mount looked ghastly. "Is this a trap?" He looked wildly about him, as if he were about to hurl himself from a window or make some similar violent gesture.

"I ain't the law," said Crook, "and if you'll take a bit of expert advice, it wouldn't do you any harm to get an official ruling on your position. Easy to see this chap's got some hold over you . . ."

"I killed my wife's first husband," said Mount, dully.

"And Kleiner's got proof? Well then, what are you

worrying about? If he's got proof of a crime and is withholding his evidence, he's guilty of bein' an accessory. Ever thought of telling him to take his evidence to Scotland Yard and be damned to him?"

"You still don't understand," exclaimed Mount. "It's not the police I'm worried about. It is my wife. I tell you, she loved that man, she believed in him. How can I wreck that faith? She has lost so much . . ."

"So that was the way of it? You really should have come to me before. You're afraid he's going to tell Mrs. Mount her husband was a phony. Well, if that's so, she can't learn it too soon."

"It would kill her," said Mount in tragic tones.

"Where does this idea come from that women are little delicate creatures that can't stand up to a storm? I tell you they're twice as tough as you or me. Look at that girl tonight, putting her head in the lion's mouth for the sake of that young chap in jail. Anyway, I never saw much sense living in a fool's paradise. Sooner or later you'll be hoofed out by the angel with the flamin' sword. Wouldn't mind acting as stand-in for him myself this once," he added.

"It's impossible," said Mount. "If you knew all the facts."

"Well, let's have some," offered Crook. "I suppose he was a member of the Party. What did he do? Sell his family down the river?"

"It could have been no one else. Only he knew where they were hidden, no one else knew the password. And she trusted him utterly. An Aryan married to a Jewess had to do something to curry favor. When

I discovered the truth—I had my contacts and I made very sure—I went to find him and kill him."

"I do like a chap who knows his own mind," approved Crook. "What happened?"

"He had wind of my coming. He was waiting for me."

"There was a little man and he had a little gun. Well, how come you weren't the corpse?"

"He was a true Nazi. He wanted his pound of flesh. He couldn't bear me to die without realizing what he'd done. He knew, I daresay, how I felt about Else, he had to have his moment of triumph. It was his vanity that cost him his life. When I grappled with him the gun went off . . ."

"Hoist on his own petard? Is that all? You know, I'll have to send you a dictionary for a Christmas present. That ain't murder, that's self-defense."

"I went there to kill him," insisted Mount monotonously.

"You might mean to leave a thousand pounds to a charity, but if you were knocked down and killed on the way to the lawyer, that wouldn't help the charity much. You're no more a murderer than me. And if you want my opinion," he added, "it wouldn't surprise me if Mrs. M. had worked that out for herself quite a while back. And even if she hasn't—well, you know what they say about the onlooker seeing most of the game—women ain't like us. They have a sort of admiration for a chap who'll risk putting his head in the noose for their sake. Hullo, sounds as if your friend's arrived."

But when the door opened it was not Kleiner but Else Mount who stood in the entry.

"You are all right?" she exclaimed to Mount. "When I found your note telling me you were coming here to meet Mr. Crook I was afraid. As for you Mr. Crook, if you really think my husband murdered his aunt . . ."

"I don't," said Crook, promptly. "He didn't murder anyone. It's all been a misunderstanding. He'll explain presently. Come in, sugar," he added over his shoulder.

Dinah James came in. "I'm not interrupting?"

Mount said, "Did he hurt you much? I had to let him make the attempt—it was our only chance—but . . ."

"You mean you knew?"

"Mr. Crook warned me there might be an attempt. I promised not to let you out of my sight."

"Let's get George in to bring us a round and then I'll do a bit of explaining," said Crook. "You know, Bastable was no fool, only he made the mistake murderers always make. They pull off one crime, or think they have, and then they can't stop. They repeat themselves. Once I knew it was him I knew he'd do his best to stop you reachin' the Seven Moons tonight, sugar. Mind you, he hadn't any idea what your evidence might be, but he wasn't going to give you a chance of passing it on."

"But I hadn't got any evidence," protested the girl.

"He wasn't to know that. I knew whoever was guilty would make the attack. Mind you, you weren't in any real danger, apart from a nasty shock and even

I couldn't save you that. We were all around you, though the job I had persuading the police to play it my way you'd never believe. Now you see why I told you to wear an extra scarf. And that was Arthur Crook lookin' after Arthur Crook. You'll be seeing Lennie again pretty soon, and I don't want to get him released on one charge of murder to be picked up within a week for another."

"He didn't hurt me, not really. I was frightened, but you promised it would be all right. I had to believe you . . ."

"Very handsome of you," said Crook, pulling out a handkerchief and trumpeting in a way that might have aroused envy in an elephant.

The drinks came in then and with them a message from Kleiner that after all it wouldn't be convenient for him to come down that evening. He'd be getting in touch.

"Wouldn't surprise me if the police get in touch with him first," observed Crook, cheerfully. "Thanks, George. Now then, any questions?"

"How did you know it was Mr. Bastable?" asked Dinah.

"In a way you could say he told me. He's like so many chaps so anxious to serve up his story with parsley around the dish that he overdoes it."

"But he had an alibi. I mean, he didn't leave his house till seven o'clock that night and Miss Foss was unconscious by that time."

"Who says he didn't?"

"Mrs. Earl saw him come out. You're not suggesting she was in it, too?"

"Of course not. Mind you, I don't blame you. I was foxed too, for a long time. Till the chap at the Ring o' Bells pointed out that the last mail goes at six-thirty. Now do you see why it was so important to find out what time Kate left the house that day?"

"Not yet."

"You're forgetting about the letter, the one Bastable wrote to the minister, sending on the figures. He didn't get those figures till five-thirty on the Friday afternoon. The Reverend got them first mail next morning, so they had to catch the six-thirty. If Kate had been in the house, well, she might have mailed the letter, but she wasn't. Ergo . . ."

"You mean, Mr. Bastable must have mailed it himself."

"Exactly. See where that leads you?"

"It means he went out *before* half past six."

"Quite. And we don't know just how long before half past six it was, though we can make a good guess. Now the invitation to the party was six-thirty and Bastable ain't a girl that has to paint his face and doll up his hair if he's going on a nice sober razzle to someone else's twenty-firster. He was back from his office before half past five because that's when the call came through. All he had to do was wash his hands and change his coat and—presto. Besides, the mailbox is some minutes' walk from his house, so why go back when he was already halfway? No one but a duck would go out for fun, unless he wanted someone to see him comin' out later on; that is, at a time when no one was going to suspect him of the murder? If Mrs. Earl hadn't been hanging around he'd have found some other chap to vouch for him, or he could have called up saying he'd be late, anything to establish an alibi. No, the way I see it he had to stop the poor lady makin' her announcement the next evening. If no one else knew what she was goin' to tell the committee, he did."

"What was he going to tell them?"

"I think quite a lot of people are goin' to have a shock when the police start making inquiries," Crook assured them. "You remember how Miss Foss was always at him to get the rebuilding job started, and he kept stalling her off? I fancy he couldn't give the word, because—well, the money wasn't there."

"Are you implying embezzlement?" asked Mount, sharply.

"More than that," said Crook, simply. "I'm stating it. You see, if I was right—and that double exit on the night of her death needed some explaining—then Miss Foss had something on Bastable that he couldn't afford to let anyone know. Tie that up with the fact that she was goin' to make a special statement to the committee the next day, and you'll see there wasn't much time left. Now you don't commit a murder, not this kind anyway, till you've reached the end of your tether and there's no other way out, so whatever it was Bastable couldn't afford to let Emily broadcast it. I'm pretty certain he was the one she was going to telephone, and he knew it. What happened next day at the committee would depend on Bastable's comeback. Now, I ain't speaking without the book. If Emily could find out something about Bastable, so could I. He dropped me a pretty broad hint that she wasn't satisfied with the way the church was bein' held up, and he had one of his moments of bravado and said to her, 'Why don't you call up the firm yourself, if you think they ain't honest?' Never dreaming, of course, that she might take him at his word."

"And she did?"

"Yes. She wrote, not long before her death, to know if the money could be raised at short notice. Signed herself secretary, said she had to make a report to her committee the following week. In return she got a letter saying there must be some mistake, they knew nothing of anyone called Bastable, and he'd made no investment through them. Presumably she should have communicated with some other firm. And they were hers, faithfully."

"How did you learn all that?" demanded Mount.

"Well, as I said, Bastable never could resist the parsley around the dish. He needn't have told the police about the call from the builders, or that he sent the figures right on to the Reverend, but he wanted to sound chummy and forthright and where was the harm? And if he hadn't told we'd never have had a thing on him. Same way, when he was telling me about Emily, he added the name of the firm, and I got Bill Parsons—that's my partner—to get in touch, find out if it was all hunky-dory, and of course he got just the same answer as Miss F., with the added information that a lady had already been in touch. Don't suppose they tied her up with the inquiry. Chaps are pretty dumb," said Mr. Candid Crook, "and it isn't as if Bastable was mentioned in the report. Anyway, the police had got their man and no sensible chap wants to tangle with the police if he can keep out of their way. Well, look how they arrest the wrong fellow and practically string him up. Only Little Miss Greatheart here saved him. Well, there you are. Miss Foss had her letter—I doubt if she showed it to Bastable, but she let him know she had it—and once the Reverend or any members of the committee had seen that, the jig was up. He had to get that back, but he had to do more. He had to shut her mouth and on my soul I don't see he had any other way of doing it unless, of course, he could raise the money and I don't think he could. Anyway she could hold it over him for the rest of his natural life and no chap could be expected to put up with that. Miss Foss had already warned Kate about looking for another job. That wasn't nosiness for once, but just tossing a hint. Because though I know we're the Welfare State and everything is a matter of glands and you can't help it really, it's still news to me that you take your housekeeper along with you when you go to jail."

"So Bastable was waiting for her by the telephone booth?" suggested Mount.

"Or in it. Don't it seem that way to you? She wouldn't yell out when she saw him, and by the time she realized what he had in mind it 'ud be too late. My guess would be she carried that letter around with her, so naturally you wouldn't look to find it in the bag when it came into Lennie Hunter's possession. Bastable 'ud have to pass by the church on his way from Newlands Court, and no one 'ud be hanging around there on a wet Friday night. Of course, he had to give the impression it was the work of a bag snatcher. No one would chuck away fifty pounds, and if he'd realized about the fiver he'd have taken that, too. I dunno about the brooch but I doubt if that ever surfaces. Probably put it where it'll never be found till Judgment Day. Then back he goes, watches his chance not to be noticed—and the fog and the rain 'ud help him there—goes in by his back door, dolls himself up, I daresay, and then hangs about till he sees Mrs. Earl, and he opens the front door, and there's your perfect alibi. And if it hadn't been her he'd have waited till someone else went by and managed to have a word with him."

"What if there had been someone else in the Court when he came? Or if Aunt Emily hadn't been alone?"

"If ifs and ans," said Crook rather impatiently. "Some risks you have to take. You ask Little Goldilocks here."

"That I cannot understand," said Mrs. Mount in a shriller voice than was normal to her. "You risked her life . . ."

"She risked her own. And anyway there was your husband and me, to say nothing of the police. Oh yes, I knew he'd be coming along to stop her mouth before she could reach the Moons, even though he didn't know what she was going to tell me. And in point of fact, of course, she hadn't got a thing. Only he believed she had, which from my point of view was just as good. Mind you, I did wonder how he was going to cover himself if anything happened to her. He couldn't say this time he was at home—at least, that's what I thought. But I was wrong. Just as I was leaving he sent a telephone message, he couldn't come, thought he'd been poisoned . . . I don't know if that was because he hoped to implicate his housekeeper. I expect we'll find she was out this evening, since he wouldn't be needing her. Anyway, he'd be sure to watch his chance, and leave the house without being seen. Then all he had to do was stop this girl from bringing her message, whatever it was, and beetle back to his bed. Who's going to say he wasn't there all the time? That was why I told George to wait five minutes and then call again. If he got a reply I was wrong. But, of course, he didn't. I'd say that call was made from a booth quite near the Common. He was lucky in his weather both times," he added. "No one's going for a walk in the snow—and it was a bit early to be coming over for drinks. Mind you, it didn't matter a tinker's curse to him who was taken for the second murder, because that's what he had in mind, there's no doubt about that, so long as Arthur Bastable was in the clear. It wouldn't surprise me to know he hasn't lost a wink of sleep since Miss Foss died. Right up to this afternoon, he never believed I'd got onto him."

"The police," began Mrs. Mount, but Crook said generously, "Don't see that you can blame them. Lennie Hunter played right into their hands. Bastable must have known someone would pick up the bag, and of course he left the fiver there on purpose. Even if the police hadn't found Lennie, it 'ud pass for a smash and grab that went a bit farther than the chap intended. No reason why they should think of our Mr. Bastable, the respected lawyer, everybody's friend, the life and soul of the party."

"So you knew all the time?" Mrs. Mount accused him. It was clear that Crook wasn't going to get off scot-free. "You knew it was Mr. Bastable, and yet you let my husband think you suspected him."

"Now don't start looking for the poisoned stilletto in your garter or wherever ladies keep it these days," Crook implored. "It's common sense in a murder to look first at the members of the family. If someone's so exasperating you have to put 'em out of the way, the people they're most likely to exasperate is their own flesh and blood. Never noticed when a lady dies sudden-like, the first person the police question is the husband even if he wasn't at home that night? And when there's money in question, as there was here, and money's needed by the other party—well, you get my point."

"So you did suspect him?" she insisted.

"Well, of course I suspected him," said Crook, reasonably. "Specially when I learned he'd been in Burtonwood that evening, and somehow forgot to inform the police. What would you have done in my shoes?"

"Is that true, Sidney? You were there?"

"I said it, didn't I?" asked Crook. "Oh yes, he was

there. And you know," he added, turning to Mount, "you didn't make things any better for yourself by not letting anyone know you'd been in Burtonwood that night."

"Is that true, Sidney?"

"Yes, Else, it's true, but I didn't see her. She had gone out already. The pity was there was no evidence I had gone to her house *after she left*."

"That's where you're wrong, chum," said Crook. "There was evidence and Miss Tremellen provided it. She heard the gate swinging later in the evening, and she thought that meant Miss Foss was back and hadn't latched it right. Maybe she thought after drinking a few healths she wasn't quite as clear-headed as usual. But we know now she never came back, and she was clear-headed enough when she left. She'd been shutting that gate firmly for upwards of forty years, so why shouldn't she latch it that one evening? And don't tell me the wind could have blown it open. It 'ud have taken a hurricane to open that gate. I know. I tried. Got some very sharp looks from the ladies, too. Thought I was tryin' to break in or something. No, it was clear to me someone had come calling after six-fifteen. You can't have missed the lady by more than a minute or two," he added, "and if it hadn't been for the weather you might even have glimpsed her sweeping into the Court. You wouldn't know about the gate, so when you left you didn't latch it proper. Now if you came after six-fifteen there were only two possibilities. One way, that your story was true; the other, that you polished off the old lady first, and then came along to the house to give yourself an air of innocence. Only in that case you'd have seen to it that someone knew you'd called and remembered the time. If no one was around, and on such a night that wasn't likely, you'd have knocked on the door of the lady next door. 'I hope my aunt's all right,' you'd have said. 'I see there's a light burning and I know she always stays in of a Friday because of the accounts, but I can't get any answer. I suppose she isn't ill or anything?' Well, that's common sense, ain't it? But you didn't even try and establish an alibi. It could be you hadn't thought of it, but it could equally be you were telling the truth, only at that stage I couldn't take any risks."

"You should have told me, Sidney," Else Mount insisted.

"I wanted to save you . . ."

"Save me? I am your wife."

"What did I tell you?" demanded Crook. "You take my tip and come clean all along the line and you won't regret it. I know when a lady means what she says," he added respectfully. "And when Mrs. M. tells you she didn't marry you just to get a British passport . . ."

"Even you cannot have believed that?" Mrs. Mount's amazement was clear to see.

"Break for five minutes, while Mr. Cupid Crook finishes his story," suggested Crook quickly. He hadn't any doubt that everything was going to be all right in that quarter from now on. "Well, I still kept an open mind about you, and then the chap at the Ring o' Bells struck a light that half blinded me. That was when he told me the last mail went out at six-thirty all around the neighborhood. After that I hadn't much doubt, but you can't offer the police a hunch, they want proof, so Bill and me and the little girl here were working like galley slaves to get it. If I'd had more time," he said almost apologetically, "I might have worked it out more dainty, but the clock was just goin' to strike and there's some risks even I don't take."

"Then—did Sidney know—this evening—that it was not he whom you expected to trap?"

"Course he knew," said Crook. "That's why I was so anxious to get him here. Bastable's a younger man than me, and it wouldn't surprise me if he was a bit quicker on his feet. I had to have someone who never took his eye off my girl, and that's what your husband was doing."

"You must have been very sure of Mr. Bastable's plan," offered Else.

"Sure I was sure. Well, it was that or a bullet through his brain, and so far as I know he don't hold a gun license."

The Mounts had gone, with Crook's professional card in Sidney's pocket.

"Next time you hear from Kleiner," said he, "show him this, telling him I'm actin' for you and I'll be glad to see him any time he cares to look in, any time at all."

The proprietor had rustled up his wife to find something for them to eat, and Crook said robustly to his young companion, "What's that? No appetite? That young fellow's like the rest of us, I suppose, doesn't want to tie up with a living skeleton. Take my word for it, sugar, what men look for isn't a girl with a figure like an anchovy fork but a nice, cozy armful. Come to that you could do with a few more pounds of flesh, and I don't care who you cut 'em from."

"What about Lennie?" Dinah clamored. "They'll have to let him out now, won't they? They haven't the right to keep him another minute."

As if she thought he might at this instant be leaving the prison walls, she laid down her knife and fork and half rose to her feet.

"Hold your horses," Crook soothed her. "He'll have to put up with a little more free board and lodging. There's formalities to be gone through . . ."

"Then I hope they'll take them at quick march," cried the girl, her face rosy with indignation. "They never had any right to take him in the first place. He ought to get compensation, or can't you bring a case against the police?"

"My guess 'ud be Lennie's had all the publicity he cares about for quite a while to come. He won't even get a chance of writing for the Sunday papers now. It's a funny thing, but once a chap's proved innocent and they know he's going to live he's a dead duck to the press. No, the one they'll be getting after will be Kate Winter. *My Twelve Years with a Murderer*. She could put by quite a nice little nest egg while she's looking for another job. No, don't tell me she won't. I know it." He sighed for the integrity of women. "Wouldn't surprise me to know she still cherishes a soft corner for him. Oh, she can be fifty and the rest, but that won't make any difference. Women go for romance from cradle to grave."

"I'm not interested in Kate's future," cried Dinah heartlessly. "She can marry him at the foot of the scaffold for all I care. It's Lennie I'm thinking of. Weeks and weeks of his life they've had. Someone ought to pay."

"Spare your indignation," Crook implored her. "Not that it don't suit you having a bit of color in your face. And don't cherish any ideas of vitriol or razor blades when the police are around. After all, they did the obvious thing, and for what we pay our police force you can't expect genius."

FOURTEEN

When they told Lennie the news he didn't believe them.

"Prison seems to warp your sense of humor," he said.

They had to bring him the newspapers before he accepted the fact that his innocence had been established. Then he threw back his head and laughed as if he'd never stop.

"Pardon me," he said at last. "Too bad of Mr. Crook, spoiling your fun. It's no wonder the cops don't like him."

"Pull yourself together, Hunter," said the warden. "You should thank God the truth's come out in time."

"Running it pretty fine, weren't you?" Lennie agreed. "As for God, I thought it was Mr. Crook."

He wasn't going to make things easy for them even now. He'd been a difficult prisoner from the start. The chaplain had never had a minute's success with him, though goodness knows he'd done his best to bring him some comfort.

"You can can that," Lennie had said. "Your lot have more in common with whoever killed Miss Foss than you'll admit. You're both murderers and you're both going to get away with it."

"Give my apologies to the hangman," he said now.

"Shame he should lose his commission. Still, I daresay you'll find some way . . ." And then he'd pitched forward in a dead faint.

While the formalities were being gone through he learned the facts, and after that he was as quiet as the grave, dangerously quiet in the guards' opinion.

"If Bastable only knew, he's lucky to be under lock and key," they confided to each other. "Hunter may not have murdered Miss Foss—well, we know he didn't—but he'd go for that fellow, given half a chance."

He had a final interview with the warden before he left the prison, but it was no more satisfactory than any of the others had been.

The warden asked him if he had any plans.

"I'll be O.K.," said Lennie.

"This Mr. Crook coming to meet you?" the warden suggested.

Lennie went white. "He better hadn't. Putting my girl through that. And I don't want any help from you," he added savagely. "I can paddle my own canoe from now on, so you needn't suggest a recommendation to a charity employer who doesn't mind giving a bad boy another chance. And I'll be all right for money, too. Get it into your head that I'm a free man, or as free as anyone can be these days. Got a free pardon, haven't I? Though pardon for what beats me? Daring to breathe, I suppose."

"Have it your own way, Hunter," said the warden. "We only want to help you."

"I've had enough of your kind of help. Thanks,"

Lennie assured him with a ghastly grin. "And look where it's nearly landed me. You and your lot have had your own way with me for weeks, months now, counting the time you kept me hanging about before the trial. Do this, go there, don't do the other, no, we can't leave you alone, no, you can't have buttons on your coat or laces in your shoes, can't eat with a knife, can't even keep your trousers up decently in case you try and strangle yourself with your suspenders, though why I should want to save you any trouble you tell me. Why don't you own up and make your peace? Haven't you got anyone you'd like to see? Questions, questions, questions, and when it wasn't you it was the press. *Lennie Hunter's Love Life. Why I killed Emily Foss. Murder doesn't pay. A message from the death cell.* Well, I'm a free man now and I don't want any more. Can't you understand a plain statement? And there's another thing. I don't want a lot of chaps hanging around with cameras when I come out. If you're so bloody keen to help, see to it no one knows the time. I'm not an old timer, this is the first time I've seen the inside of a prison, and you can bet your sweet life it'll be the last. I want to be left alone to get on with things my own way. I'm not a two-headed freak and I didn't catch a silly old woman around the throat and choke her life out in a dark alley for the sake of her money bags. And if the newspapers want to know what it feels like to be graciously pardoned for something you didn't do, well, I never learned to write. That's good enough for them."

They gave him back everything that had been in his

pockets when they brought him in, they gave him his own clothes. He put everything just where he'd always kept it, shook hands with the guards, but not the chaplain or the warden, and said, "First time I've ever stayed anywhere where they haven't asked for the rent." Then he marched out. They'd kept the time of his departure a secret, and there were no newspapermen waiting for him. He threw a sharp glance left and right; the street was nearly empty. There was a café not far off and he thought about dropping in, then realized they'd guess he came from the prison, so he stuck his hands in his pockets and strolled past on the other side of the road. A door opened and Dinah came out. She wasn't wearing jeans this morning, but a skirt with a long blue coat over it, and her smooth head was bare. Funny how it took the glancing sunlight that was breaking through the clouds. He hadn't noticed that before. She came calmly across the road and slipped an arm through his. He made as if to jerk away, but he couldn't, not without hurting her. He didn't want to do that. They walked for a short time in silence. At last he said, "Where are we going?"

"I don't know," said Dinah. "I'm leaving that to you."

"Is it true," asked Lennie suddenly, "that—that—that you nearly got yourself killed?"

"Oh, I was all right," said Dinah instantly. "Mr. Crook was looking after me."

"I'll have a word to say to him," promised Lennie dangerously. "Set a trap with you as bait, all so that he could get his name in the papers, I suppose. He's going to do a bit of explaining before the day's out, and for his own sake, let's hope it's good."

"Happy to oblige," said a voice in his ear. Lennie nearly jumped out of his skin. They had turned a corner while they were talking and now for the first time both perceived the big ancient Rolls, its yellow coachwork taking the light gallantly, drawn up by the curb.

Mr. Crook's huge face beamed at them through an open window.

"Joined the circus?" asked Lennie, rudely.

"Why?" asked Crook. "Were you thinking they might give you a job?"

Lennie stiffened. "I can look after myself," he said.

"Maybe," said Crook, but not as though he believed it. "How about looking after the little lady for a change?"

Lennie glared. "If you'd let anything happen to her I'd have been jugged for a real murder," he said.

"There's times you have to take chances," offered Crook, mildly.

"That's your affair," Lennie retorted. "I'm talking about Dinah taking chances."

"This time next year," offered Crook, leaning out and opening the rear door of the car, "you meet me any place you name and if you've found any way of stopping dames taking chances—I—I'll give you the Old Superb. Well, if you ain't coming my way, I fancy the little lady is. Come in alongside me, sugar, and we'll have one for the road on the way."

Lennie caught his girl by the arm and propelled her into the car.

"You'll sit with me," he said. "Haven't you got yourself into trouble enough, as it is?"

"Spoken like a husband," said Crook heartily. He slammed his own door and threw in the clutch.

In perfect amity the three drove toward London.

The End

>>> If you've enjoyed this book and would like to discover more great vintage crime and thriller titles, as well as the most exciting crime and thriller authors writing today, visit: >>>

The Murder Room
Where Criminal Minds Meet

themurderroom.com

>>

www.ingramcontent.com/pod-product-compliance
Ingram Content Group UK Ltd.
Pitfield, Milton Keynes, MK11 3LW, UK
UKHW022316280225
455674UK00004B/329